PRAISE FOR ENTROMANCY: BOOK ONE OF THE NIGHTPATH TRILOGY

"Entromancy is that rare gem you find among the all-too-common dross of self-published novels. Author M. S. Farzan takes a premise that is truly unique and imaginative . . . throws in a diverse cast of characters, all to deliver an urban fantasy thrill ride."

--San Francisco Book Review

"In this rousing...science fiction novel, it's a futuristic San Francisco and the element [c]eridium has emerged as a renewed source of mythical power and otherworldly strength. Ceridium's side-effects, however, unlock mutative genes in the population resulting in a secondary race called [a]urics who become threatening to the human population. Thankfully, vigilant cops like Eskander Aradowsi are defending the races and reinforcing the safety of each. The narrative is fast-paced...this is a promising...launching point for the planned series."

--The BookLife Prize in Fiction

"Entromancy has been an amazing journey...which I think I would like to take again

in the next book of the Nightpath Trilogy. The world building is out of this world no pun intended. If you like a lot of action, fighting and guns a blazing then you are going to fall in love with this series."

--The Avid Reader

"ENTROMANCY has one of the coolest speculative fiction worlds I've encountered in a while. The mix of magic and technology is an amazing blend that results in all kind of badassery from the characters. Backdropped against a sort of dystopian/Philip Marlow-ian cityscape, it felt like an epic D&D slipstream universe...I recommend this book for anyone who wants to get lost in an awesome world and/or anyone who grew up on table-top role-playing games."

--Kit 'N Kabookle

"I love all the characters in the book...I love the little hint of romance that floats in the plot while everyone get shot at. I really couldn't put this book down once it got started."

--Emily Carrington

"This book was a fun to read story that centered on several important issues concerning diversity, differences, and deeply-held fears. I read mostly to be entertained, but I couldn't help but think about some of problems in terms of today's

political climate. An attention-grabbing tale of conspiracy, hatred, and misconceptions that was easy to read, fresh, and frightening, my reading time was well-spent with this book."

--Laurie's Paranormal Thoughts and Reviews

"I am in love with the worldbuilding on this one. Seriously, it's amazing. It's hard to write science fiction with fantasy races and have it make sense, but by jove, I have now seen it done...I'd recommend picking this up if you like a good mix of science fiction and fantasy."

--Where Landsquid Fear to Tread

"I enjoyed the story a great deal...The plot was tense and also topical, which was a great boon to the book. I liked the way that current events were used to see a new race and a new world order."

--Judge, 25th Annual Writer's Digest Self-Published Book Awards

"Very vivid...Very compelling...Very fresh and punchy"

--Judge, 5th Annual Writer's Digest Self-Published eBook Awards

PRAISE FOR ENTROMANCY: A CYBERPUNK FANTASY RPG

"An agile little assassin...Entromancy is a gem waiting to be found."

--Geek Native

"I am seriously impressed with this book. My favorite part is the near-total absence of scaling, and the menu-option approach to gaining new features from your class and destiny. It works well here for the same reason it works well in Powered by the Apocalypse playbooks and 13th Age."

--Tribality

"Nightpath [Publishing] has established a setting with teeth that can grab the imagination of player and game master."

--EN World

"A...cyberpunk/fantasy take on the 5E rules that might be one of the fastest pick-up-and-play games out there."

--Drop Lowest

BOOKS BY M. S. FARZAN

Entromancy: Book One of the Nightpath Trilogy
Technomancy: Book Two of the Nightpath Trilogy
Shadowmancy: Book Three of the Nightpath Trilogy
Jinnspeak

GAMES BY M. S. FARZAN

Entromancy: A Cyberpunk Fantasy RPG
Entromancy: Hacker Battles
Not-So-Super Villains

TECHNOMANCY

BOOK TWO OF THE NIGHTPATH TRILOGY

M. S. Farzan

For my parents
Who read, comment, critique,
and unfailingly, support

KEY LOCATIONS

AURICHOME – Squatting less than forty miles from San Francisco proper in what's known as the "North Bay," the nation of Aurichome is a haven for all races - provided that they swear unequivocal fealty to King Thog'run II. Parts of the underground kingdom are still under construction, but its borders are ever-expanding, and well-defended.

COLUMBUS-FARROW – The carnivalesque atmosphere of the city's North Beach district is punctuated by booming music, kaleidoscopic three-dimensional digital ads ("digads"), and neon lights. If there's action to be had, it can undoubtedly be found here.

DOWNTOWN – San Francisco, being geographically contained within a forty-nine-square-mile peninsula, was one of the first global city centers to begin building vertically in earnest. The skyline is crowded to the point of being impenetrable to all but the midday sun, and the auric-majority undercity reaches half as deep into the earth as Downtown's tallest building.

EAST BAY – What the East Bay lacks in glamor, it more than makes up for in diversity. Industrial shipyards and towering skyscrapers can be found alongside luxury houses and underground ghettos, and there are rumors of safehouses and saloons located in abandoned subway train stations.

GOLDEN GATE BRIDGE – The iconic suspension bridge lay dormant and decrepit for a period of two decades, caught in the crossfire between Aurichome to the north and the Pacific South NIGHT headquarters. It has since been returned to its former glory as a tremulous show of peace between the two factions, serving as an orange beacon spanning the San Francisco Bay.

NEW CASTRO – Rivaled only by Columbus-Farrow in its ostentation, the centrally located New Castro is home to nightclubs, digad-pocked virtual reality emporiums, and vacation suites. It's sleek, it's sexy, and it represents the absolute best that San Francisco money can buy.

PACIFIC SOUTH NIGHT HEADQUARTERS – Poised forebodingly on the island of Alcatraz in the center of the San Francisco Bay, the three ivory towers of the Pacific South NIGHT headquarters house over two hundred NIGHT agents, Inquisitors, foot soldiers, staff, and officials. It has enough space for fifty virtual penitentiary inhabitants, and is comparable in size to the Pacific North NIGHT headquarters in Seattle, Central West NIGHT headquarters in Denver, and Atlantic North NIGHT headquarters in New York.

PRESIDIO – Once a military base, then a park, now an overgrown forest that abuts the Golden Gate Bridge to the north, the Presidio is a not-so-mute testament to the societal and magical issues that plague modern societies. Filled with ragers and worse, the Presidio has been reported to feature a naturally occurring source of ceridium, although no faction has yet been publicly willing to send its forces to investigate.

RICHMOND-SUNSET DISTRICT – Ordinary people have to find somewhere to live, and in San Francisco, the Richmond-Sunset District is their best option. Soaring apartment buildings, underground housing structures, and the ever-present dual layer of traffic all dot the landscape, along with a visibly Aurichome-themed sports bar known as *They Might Be Giant*.

SANTA CLARA – Having boomed and busted multiple times over, Silicon Valley has continued to expand, finding Santa Clara to be its current hub forty-five miles south of San Francisco. All manner of technology - from drones and antigravity cars to cerujet engines and ceridium weaponry - can be found here, provided that one has the appropriate connections and pay grade.

SPARKS, NV – Two hundred and twenty miles to the east of San Francisco, beyond a dwarven outpost and the forgotten - but still neon - city of Reno, sits the tiny city of Sparks, Nevada. From this suburb appeared an augur known as the Sigil, who has since taken up residence in an open-air casino amphitheater in Reno, surrounded by drones and all types of machinery.

KEY PERSONAE

AGRID THE DESTROYER – A low auric entromancer and known equally as "the Destroyer" and "the Betrayer," Agrid once had the command of a legion of assassins loyal to his word alone, although he has spent the past year languishing in the dungeons of Aurichome.

ALINA "THE PITCHER" HADZIC – Former relief pitcher and owner of a revolutionary-friendly tavern in the Richmond-Sunset District known as *They Might Be Giant*, Alina Hadzic is a veteran high auric terramancer and Aurichome's official Consul for Human-Auric Relations.

ESKANDER ARADOWSI – Spymaster to the king, Eskander Aradowsi holds the dubious honor of being one of the first high auric NIGHT agents, having recently made the jump to Aurichome after a mission gone south.

GLORIC VUNDERFEL – Gloric Vunderfel is a gnome technomancer extraordinaire and King Thog'run's Chief of Technology, despite his long-standing ties with the Sigil of Sparks.

MARGUERITE LIU – Former attaché to William D. Karthax, Marguerite "Madge" Liu is a human

Daypath of some repute and voted to be the next Inquisitor General after her predecessor abdicated the position under accusations of treason.

THE SIGIL OF SPARKS – Although the artificial intelligence experiment has failed many times over, rumors boast of a sentient, preternaturally clairvoyant leader who, just as strangely, takes the form of an early-twentieth century automatic vacuum cleaner and is attended only by his cantankerous - and very human - Scribe.

STRIKER JOHNSON – Striker Johnson is a NIGHT agent celebrated for his efforts during the Karthax affair, although his metal arm, breastplate, and assortment of cybernetics indicate the toll the incident has taken on the human Nightpath.

THOG'RUN II – A low auric war hero and sovereign of Aurichome, King Thog'run II is known far and wide for his battle prowess, tactical acumen, and brutal dealings with enemies of the throne.

TRIBE ACHEBE – A high auric vanguard and the adoptive nephew of King Thog'run, Tribe Achebe is more often found causing problems for Aurichome than solving them.

VASSHKA "DOUBLESHOT" LESTRAGE –
Known by most only by her moniker,
"Doubleshot," the dwarf Vasshka Lestrage is a
revolutionary in service to the crown and one of
King Thog'run's personal tactical advisors.

WILLIAM D. KARTHAX – (location unknown) A
war hero and the former Inquisitor General of
NIGHT, William D. Karthax was indicted *in
absentia* for collusion against NIGHT while
attempting to manipulate King Thog'run and
Aurichome. Karthax was last seen escaping
from the Pacific South NIGHT headquarters on
Alcatraz.

PROLOGUE

Andrew Alyawarre hung his head in his hands, desperate. The figure on the holodisplay in front of him continued to speak, filling the small hotel room with its androgynous monotone.

"This does not have to be difficult, auromancer," the voice said dispassionately. "Complete the task to our satisfaction, and she will be released into your custody."

The big man sat up straight, letting his curly black hair slip through brown fingertips. He squinted at the holodisplay, staring as though his eyesight could penetrate the vaguely humanoid form on the screen. Several acerbic retorts came to his mind, but he knew that the representative on the other side of the holodisplay – whoever it was, and wherever they were – would not take kindly to his sarcasm.

Andrew spoke honestly. "At what cost?" His voice, ordinarily deep and smooth, was hoarse with emotion.

"The question is not of cost, auromancer, but of ability," the holodisplay voice responded quickly, misunderstanding his question. "If you can perform the task adequately, the repercussions will be of no concern to you.

"I will send the coordinates to your digitab immediately," the figure continued. "Utilize the credit account you have been provided for any necessary transactions."

The holodisplay flashed once, illuminating the sparsely furnished room in brightness, then fell dim. Andrew sat in the darkness, staring at the empty holodisplay, his mind half a world away. The vertical metal cylinder that housed the machine's innards offered him no answers, and the sparsely furnished room was quiet except for the continuous buzz of traffic coming from the single-pane windows.

The man slowly let his head fall back into his giant hands, and wept.

*****

Damara Drivas liked baseball more than she liked magic, but while one was a hobby, the other kept the lights on. She kept the midday game tracker running on her lens display while she worked, directing her attention now and then to the corner of her vision to keep up with the score and highlights.

"Our issue is not with his eligibility, Inquisitor," the party representative repeated, drawing Damara's attention away from the game-in-progress statistics. "But with his status. Neither the NIGHTs nor the federal government know where Karthax *is*. Otherwise, I'm sure they would have court martialed him by now."

Damara let her gaze rest on the politician, expertly masking her contempt for his feeble attempt at drawing information from her to bolster his position. She looked at him blankly, her warm brown eyes inscrutable, and rested her cheek on a delicate hand as though considering her next comment with great care.

Expertly, she pierced a small blue stone set within her earring with a finger, allowing a tiny gasp of azure vapor to escape from within, unnoticed by the oblivious man in front of her. She allowed the silence to stretch between them uncomfortably as the ceridium vapor snuck its way through her nostrils and into her body, silently empowering her with the means with which to work her craft. When she spoke next, it was with power.

"Let *us* concern ourselves with finding the Inquisitor General," Damara said at last, her dulcet tones having a hypnotic effect on the hapless politician. She could see his eyes glaze over subtly as the magic took hold, snaking through his subconscious and nudging him ever so gently to respond more agreeably to her.

"And while we do that," she continued, confident in her ability to sway the weak-willed politician, "your factors will set the stage for his triumphant return to the political circuit."

The fat man nodded slowly, his jowls bouncing as any vestiges of resistance to the stunningly beautiful woman sitting across from him fell away. Somehow, he felt as though he could trust her, and that her ideas, while across party lines from his own, would benefit him in some way.

"I'll do it," he said, "although I can't promise compliance from everyone else."

Damara smiled a winning smile, allowing herself the slightest bit of pride in how easily the meeting had turned in her favor. She sat back in her chair, the waves of her dark brown hair cascading down her shoulders.

"Let us concern ourselves with that as well," she said again reassuringly, tightening the noose around the politician's mind with her magically enhanced voice.

The man nodded again mutely, inspired by the conversation and unaware of the magical intervention. He rose to leave, allowing the Inquisitor to peer again at the statistics on her lens display.

A fielding error during play had allowed the opposing team to score, putting them ahead in the bottom of the eighth inning. Bases were loaded, with no outs.

Damara sighed irritably at the politician's back as he left the room.

*****

Kwame Daigan climbed, and kept climbing. The trail to the mountain fortress had been eroded by time, and was no more than a suggestion carved into the near-vertical cliff face.

His strong, dark hands knew the mountain well enough, and his aging but powerful legs propelled him ever forward. A long, embroidered jacket lined with white Tibetan lamb wool protected him from the cold wind that pressed him against the rocks. A wrapped package, as big as his torso, was strapped to his shoulders with twine, still warm even in the plummeting temperature.

Soon enough, he reached the cave opening,

stepping surely around the rocky entrance and onto the smoother path within. The wind stopped abruptly as he entered the grotto, reduced to a plaintive howl behind him. The cave was cool and damp, with the faint aroma of brimstone and something more metallic, which to anyone else would have seemed pungent, if not slightly revolting.

To the auric, it smelled like home.

He shifted the package on his shoulders and marched forward, through the small passage and into a massive cavern, carved from the same stone as the mountain encasing it, but with walls that had been smoothed as though with a giant spoon. The grotto lacked a ceiling, allowing the evening starlight to bathe the area with radiance. Precious and semi-precious crystals sparkled in the dim light, veins of splendor within the silky grey stone that was marred only by scorch marks at intervals along the walls.

At the center of the cavern lay an enormous beast, a dark and foreboding presence in the otherwise wondrous cave. It was coiled like a snake, its front and rear paws tucked beneath its massive girth and its triangular tail framing its muscular body. Two black wings sat folded across its back, and a horned, angular head rested upon the stone floor towards the cave opening. Here and there, a metallic scale on the beast's body glittered from the starlight, easily as brilliant as the crystals set within the walls.

"What have you brought?" the beast asked, its multi-toned voice booming across the cavern walls. Although spoken at no more than a whisper, the question still shook the mountain, requiring Kwame to set his feet firmly beneath him.

"Dinner," the shadowmancer replied, untying the package from his shoulders and dropping it in front of the dragon. He unwrapped it carefully, revealing a medium-sized mountain goat that had been freshly killed and drained of blood.

The dragon's eyes remained closed, but it inhaled through a nostril the size of Kwame's head.

"Not even breakfast," the beast taunted, exhaling. A gust as strong as the outside wind, but smelling of fire and metal, hit Kwame squarely in the chest, causing him to take a step backward.

"No appreciation from an old fool," the shadowmancer replied testily.

One of the dragon's eyes opened at that, its nictitating membrane sliding back to reveal a sparkling green orb spattered with flecks of gold. "Only an old fool expects appreciation for that which is his duty."

The silence held, as did the dragon's gaze, boring into Kwame like a green and gold laser.

The shadowmancer broke first, laughing harshly into the dimness. "My apologies, Zzethromandus. This was all I could find on the way here," he explained.

The dragon guffawed as well, a grating, bellowing sound in the hollow cavern. "No harm, old friend," it said reassuringly. "It shall be my breakfast."

Ponderously, the beast pushed itself up onto its forelegs, opening its other eye and shaking its wings free from slumber. It moved its head from side to side and opened its considerable maw in what looked like a yawn, revealing rows of dagger-like teeth.

Without preamble, Zzethromandus darted his arrow-shaped head towards the mountain goat, plucking it from the floor delicately with his front teeth. He flexed his powerful neck to toss it upwards, then caught it deftly in his open mouth. The dragon bit down once, scissoring meat, bones, and fur within his maw, then swallowed the rest of the animal whole.

Kwame stood politely, ignoring the sickening sounds emanating from the dragon's mouth and the bits of blood and bone that rained down in front of him.

At length, Zzethromandus eyed him piercingly. "What do you want?" the dragon rumbled.

The shadowmancer cleared his throat. "A war is coming," he said openly, knowing that the dragon would see through any prevarication. "It is time."

Zzethromandus picked at his giant teeth with an equally long and yellow forenail. "You orichites and humans are always warring about something, if not the other," he boomed.

"We prefer 'aurics,'" Kwame boldly corrected the dragon, whose knowledge of humanoid species was centuries old and in clear need of an update. "And this war will be of the kind that will arrive at even your doorstep, if you don't act upon it presently."

The dragon cocked its head to the side, considering. He looked at Kwame like a giant bird examining its prey.

"It has been long, by human and dragon

standards, since I went to war," Zzethromandus said thoughtfully.

"Let's hope it doesn't come to that," Kwame replied quickly. "If it does, I'll need much more than just your help."

The dragon laughed again, a terrible sound. "Since when did you become so unruly, Kwame Daigan?"

The shadowmancer sighed, wiping his forehead with a swarthy hand. "I'm just tired, and old," he said.

"What does that make me?" the dragon asked wryly.

ONE

"I'm not here to talk about auric rights; I'm here to talk about baseball. We've got three more to play in this series and I'm just trying to win games for this team. If you want to talk politics, you can ask me in the off-season; if you want to ask a question about baseball, ask."

-Alina Hadzic, post-game interview during the
2068 Global Series

The door buzzer beeped, a merciful reprieve from the constant racket. I rummaged through the couch cushions, extricating my forgotten digitab and pushing a button to answer the intercom.

"Yeah?" I said, putting the digitab up to one ear and a finger in the other to block out some of the sound.

"Eskander?" Alina's voice buzzed through the digitab's speaker. "Are you there?"

"Hey! Hang on," I replied, ducking out of my living room and out of the way of a soapy sponge flying out of the kitchen. "Sorry, what's up?"

"You haven't answered your phone in two

days," she admonished. "I came by to make sure everything's alright."

I shut the living room door behind me, muffling the cacophony of yelling, television noise, and banging of pots and pans. The skinny entryway of my apartment was a disaster, and I stepped around a morass of shoes, umbrellas, toys, and not a few shopping bags towards the front door.

"Yeah, sorry," I repeated, pulling the digitab away from my stubbled face. "It's kind of a mess here."

I heard Alina sigh into the intercom, and felt a little guilty. "How are you?" I managed weakly.

"Fine," she said curtly. "Are you going to let me in?"

"Sure," I said dubiously, looking down at my undershirt and sweatpants. I wasn't expecting company. "Are you downstairs?"

"I'm outside your apartment," the Pitcher growled, exasperated. I could almost hear her eyes rolling at me. "You gave me the passcode to the building, remember?"

"Right, right," I said, jumping as a shoe or some other object hit the living room door behind me. "Just a second."

I clicked off the intercom through the digitab, looking down the long hallway that ran parallel to my apartment's front wall. A large, sunburst-shaped mirror hung at the far wall to my left, at the end of a corridor that led to the place's only bathroom. The image that greeted me was little better than the chaotic entryway, and more disheveled. My normally brown hair was almost black from not being washed in several days, sticking out to one side unfashionably. My pointed nose and angular cheekbones were comically accentuated by my three-day beard, and dark half-circles could be seen under my brown eyes even at this distance. My slightly pointed ears poked out awkwardly, making my neck look abnormally long, and although my body was tanned and muscular under my shirt, I had undeniably gained a few pounds.

I brushed a hand perfunctorily through my hair, which only swept it from one side to the other, and hastily grabbed a grey zip-up sweatshirt from the pile at my feet, thrusting my hands through it and dropping the digitab. I stepped over a rubber skateboard and punched a number into the front door's security system, turning the key that was already sitting in the physical lock.

I opened the door as nonchalantly as I could, leaning on the frame and trying to use my body to hide the clutter behind me.

"How's it going?" I said casually.

The Pitcher glared at me, her blue eyes gleaming, and lips pursed in irritation. A wayward curl framed the left side of her face under her baseball cap, and she wore a simple blue jumper and tight jeans.

"Fine," she said for a second time, looking me up and down. Her look softened somewhat as she saw my condition, laugh lines creasing slightly at her eyes. "Better than you, I guess."

"It's been rough," I said honestly.

Her brow furrowed as she took in my outfit, and I noticed that my sweatshirt felt a little snug. I realized belatedly that it was a woman's jacket, and two sizes too small. I was not covering myself in glory.

"Can I come in?" she asked.

"Um," I hesitated. The living room door opened behind me, letting in a clamor of voices and mechanical sounds. A short, portly woman with graying hair stuck her head into the hall, putting a soapy wet hand on the outer doorknob.

"Eskander," she said, "will you *please* tell your sister that her children can*not* play in the kitchen while I'm..."

Her voice trailed off as she saw Alina, standing perplexed in the doorway. The woman looked from her, to me, and back again, equally taken aback.

"Who's this, Eskander?" she said imperiously.

I hung my head, defeated. "Mom," I said, uncomfortable, "this is Alina. Alina, this is my mother."

"Oh, *really*," my mother said without missing a beat, her tone simultaneously warm and inviting towards Alina and admonishing towards me. "I have heard so very little about someone so very pretty!" she said, entering the hallway and wiping her hands on the corner of her apron.

"It's nice to meet you, Mrs. Aradowsi," the Pitcher said smoothly, extending her hand.

My mother grabbed it greedily, pulling Alina in for a hug, which the half-auric returned politely. She then hooked an arm around the Pitcher's elbow, steering her towards the living room door.

"Arabiyya-Ferdowsi," the older woman

corrected, shooting a withering glance in my direction. "*Some* of us are not ashamed of our heritage."

"Mom, I..." I protested.

"Come, dear!" my mother continued, ushering Alina through the doorway. "You could not have come at a more perfect time. The whole family is here!"

A deluge of sounds flooded through the open door, children's voices mixed with the blaring of sports noise and TV announcing. I looked over at the sunburst mirror once again, shaking my head at my reflection, and followed my mother and Alina into the room.

What was ordinarily a tidy living room had devolved into complete chaos. An uncountable number of toys were strewn haphazardly around the floor, and a fort made from couch cushions partially blocked the entrance to the kitchen to the left. Empty juice containers and snack pouches littered nearly every furniture surface, and three of the room's several digital art frames stood askew against the cream walls, pushed askance by tiny, sticky hands. Two small children jumped up and down on a small loveseat to the right, yelling unintelligibly at one another, while a young woman, holding a tiny baby, tried to interpose herself between them. Across the room, an older man sat on a cushionless couch watching the giant augmented reality TV in the corner, seemingly oblivious to the bedlam.

"Artin," my mother called to the man, holding onto Alina's arm like a vise. Receiving no response, she tried again, louder. "Artin! *ART!*"

The man started, looking over, surprise in his

almond-shaped eyes. His balding brown head still had several strings of grey hair, which did nothing to hide his long ears.

"What is it, Beybun?" he protested. "The Union are up two-nil!"

"Bah, turn it down," my mother demanded, nearly shouting over the television noise and children arguing. "We have a guest!"

The sight of Alina was like a hot knife through butter in the frenzy. My father's eyes narrowed as he put together the pieces, and he reached a hand out to tap the digital console embedded in the couch's armrest, muting the ARTV. The younger woman turned from admonishing her children, stopping in mid-sentence and looking at us quizzically. Even the boy and girl stopped their jumping and yelling.

"Art, Suzan, this is Alina," my mother said into the sudden silence, gesturing at the Pitcher beside her. "Eskander's *friend*," she added meaningfully.

My father was the first to react, springing spryly from the couch to shake Alina's hand, deftly freeing her from my mother's grasp. "Nice to meet you, nice to meet you," he said in slightly accented English. "My daughter, Suzan," he waved a hand towards the younger woman behind him.

Alina reached her hand out to my sister, who managed to clasp it around the baby in her arms.

"Hi," Suzan greeted her warmly, her face changing instantly from chiding mother to friendly host. "We've heard so much - and not enough! - about you," she said, glaring past

Alina at me.

I made a face at her and walked over to the ARTV, passing a hand over a separate console and putting it to sleep. My father looked over at me accusingly, more interested in the soccer match than the current discussion. I waved at him angrily, gesturing towards Alina and my sister, which earned me a grunt of mixed irritation and resignation.

"Thank you," Alina said genuinely, reflexively adjusting her baseball cap. "I have to say the same, as Eskander speaks about his family quite often." I beamed at that, looking at my mother pointedly.

The Pitcher leaned down to look at the two rugrats, who were suddenly shy, peeking out from behind my sister's legs. "This must be Perinaz and Alex," she said, smiling at them. They looked at her curiously, their eyes large and softly pointed ears twitching.

"Yes, and Memet," Suzan answered for them, offering the cooing baby. "Would you like to hold him?"

"Sure," Alina said dubiously, taking him into her arms.

"Suzan, will you help me in the kitchen please?" my mother asked pointedly.

"Yes, mother," my sister said, giving Alina a winning smile. The two children followed her, looking back more than once at the Pitcher.

We stood there awkwardly in the suddenly quiet room, Alina bouncing my tiny nephew upon her chest, and my father looking from her, to the augmented reality television, and back again. I cleared my throat and gestured towards the loveseat.

"Want to sit down?" I offered.

Alina looked up from Memet, seeming to have gotten the hang of holding him. She nodded politely.

I walked her over to the small sofa, snatching a model cerujet sticking out from in between the cushions and placing it carefully on a side table. The Pitcher sat down gingerly, still gently bobbing the baby, who seemed content for the moment.

My father had taken up his post on the cushionless couch, his liver-spotted hand hovering longingly near the ARTV console built into the couch arm. I crossed the small ocean of toys to join him, brushing the plain fabric beneath me perfunctorily, trying to sweep it free from crumbs. The older man looked up at me quizzically as I sat down, and I sighed, nodding my acquiescence.

Energized, he waved a hand over the couch arm, and the ARTV burst into life, its centi-core ceridium processor instantly displaying the in-progress match in full 5D. Twenty-two soccer players appeared on a vibrantly green pitch in front of the ARTV, their three-dimensional holograms hovering several feet off the floor. A recognizable bouquet of grass, freshly draughted beer, and the unmistakable tang of sweat wafted through the room as the ARTV's pheromone adapter simulated the smells of the stadium. The couch and loveseat, connected through the network to the ARTV's motion simulator, vibrated and pulsed with each kick of the ball, and every contact between players. The sounds of players yelling, sportscasting, and ambient crowd noise assaulted our ears, causing me to wince. Even Memet burbled loudly in protest.

I pushed a button on the console embedded on my side of the couch, dialing down the non-visual stimuli to a less offensive level. The roar of the stadium reduced to a muffled din, while the couches rumbled considerably more softly and the pheromone adapter consolidated the ambient aromas to a single faint odor of lawn shavings.

"Still two-nil," my father said quietly, reading the score banner that floated above the moving players. Having lived the first thirty years of his life in Eurasia, and the following forty on the East Coast, he was both a dedicated soccer fan and an uncompromising Philadelphia Union supporter. Being a relatively recent retiree, he was loath to commit to any activities on what he simply called "matchday," which had already provided for a number of scheduling mishaps during my family's visit. It didn't help that neither my mother nor my sister shared his love for the game, or sport in general, and took the brunt of his intricately detailed explanations of which midfielders were to be sold to whose team, and what the ensuing tactics should be. I, on the other hand, had inherited the sport gene, and so had my sister's children, but even we had our limits.

"So," my father said abruptly, and a bit too loud for the small room. "Eskander tells me you are a diplomat of some sort?"

"That's right," Alina replied, smiling charmingly above Memet's tiny head. "I'm the Consulate to Aurichome here in San Francisco."

"Uh huh," my father said, not really listening.

"And when did you start doing that?"

"About a year ago, when your son became King Thog'run's Chief of Intelligence."

"Uh huh."

The Pitcher, seasoned from years spent in the media limelight and a bartender besides, was an expert at getting people to talk. She shifted Memet on her shoulder and tugged on a sock that he had been trying to kick off.

"What do you think about Philly's chances for playoff berth this year?"

My father looked across the room at her, as though seeing her for the first time. "Pretty good," he said slowly, gauging her interest. "If they can get their back four to hold a line longer than two minutes."

"Their defense is spotty," Alina agreed, "but they need to stop hoofing long balls over the top if they want to start dictating pace and possession."

"Exactly!" my father exclaimed, excited to have someone with whom he could talk shop. "You're from around here, so tell me this: why haven't the Earthquakes fired their manager after seven-"

"Lunch is ready!" my mother chirped cheerily, bustling into the living room with an enormous tray of plates and bowls, all covered with heat-containing polymer tins.

My sister followed her, shuttling a trestle table that had been moved to the kitchen to make way for the pillow fort. She was taller than me, and thinner, but had the dark hair and swarthy complexion that all of us shared from our Kurdish heritage. She took more after my grandmother's auric gene than I did, the tips of her long, pointed brown ears almost touching the side of her head. Not expecting company, she was still dressed casually in a grey sweat suit, minus the zip-up hoodie that I was now wearing.

Perinaz and Alex followed her in from the kitchen, uncharacteristically quiet. With the addition of Alina to the small lunch party, my sister and mother had undeniably lectured my niece and nephew about being on their best behavior, which was sure to last for at least two minutes. Perinaz, the older one, was the spitting image of her mother, save for the bouncy curls that framed her angular face. Alex took more after his father, who had stayed in Philadelphia to look after his burgeoning digitab application business. The little boy had a mischievous, round face with tousled chestnut hair, and clung shyly to his sister's sleeve.

"Alina, I do hope you like our food," my mother said, waiting patiently for Suzan to set up the trestle table amidst the sea of toys. Satisfied that my sister had placed the table on a solitary patch of even ground, she set down the tray, handing me a bundle of plateware to distribute.

"Oh," Alina said politely, readjusting a now-sleeping Memet on her shoulder, "I'm sure I will love Kurdish food-"

"Cheesesteaks!" my mother exclaimed. She began snatching polymer tins from the plates and bowls and stashing them under the table, revealing a ridiculous spread of fresh buns, cooked beef, pressurized cheese, and innumerable condiments.

Ordinarily, the rest of the family would have descended upon the meal like a band of rabid animals, but with a new guest, the mood was considerably tempered. I got up to hand out plates and napkins, and my father tore himself away from the match long enough to help himself to a cheesesteak with fixings. My sister offered to take Memet from Alina, who complied gratefully, smoothing her shirt and joining the rest of the family in putting together lunch.

When everyone had prepared their respective plates – my mother looking after Perinaz and Alex, who were particularly fussy about their food – my father resumed his perch nearest to the ARTV, and my mother took my seat on the cushionless couch. I sat in between them, while Suzan excused herself to put Memet in for a nap. Perinaz made herself comfortable in the entryway to the pillow fort, looking a little like a wolf pup in front of her den. Alex sat down bravely next to Alina on the loveseat, staring at her with his round hazel eyes and ignoring, for what may have been the first time in his life, the food in front of him.

"Are you my uncle's girlfriend?" he asked suddenly.

To her credit, Alina didn't flinch at the question, and instead looked across the room at me over her plate. "I don't know, Alex," she said impishly, still staring at me. "Why don't you ask your uncle?"

I coughed around a mouthful of cheesesteak, nearly spilling my lunch. I was wholly unprepared for this conversation alone with Alina, not to mention with my entire family present.

"Now, now, Lexi," said my mother, using my nephew's nickname. "It's not polite to ask people about their relationships." I was skeptical, knowing that I would receive an earful about the topic when Alina wasn't within earshot.

"Are you a half-auric like pop pop?" Perinaz peeped from the pillow fort, her high cheeks already smattered with cheese.

"I am," Alina said, giving the little girl a winning smile. "My father is an auric, just like your great-grandmother."

Seemingly satisfied with her response, Perinaz resumed devouring her child-sized sandwich. Suzan returned from putting Memet to bed, and stooped over the table to prepare lunch for herself.

"Alina," she said warmly, "how did you and Eskander first meet?"

My sister and I ordinarily get along famously. Having grown up in three different countries, two of which were still auric-human warzones, we learned to rely on each other in the way that only children of war can know. Our parents, who had been raised during times of relative peace, were able to cope with the auric revolutions that had rocked modern Kurdistan, Ukraine, and countless other countries in the thirties and forties. Suzan and I still retained some of that survivor mentality running from refugee camp to camp, thinking of home as a transient place and clinging to one another, and our family, instead of locations.

Once in a good while, however, she would say something that pushed a button in the way that only siblings could do. In one seemingly earnest question she had put Alina on the spot, prompting her to reveal the underside of her early days working as a fence for the revolutionary kingdom of Aurichome.

"Suzan..." I began, reproach in my voice.

"At *They Might Be Giant*," Alina interrupted me, referring to the sports bar that she had owned since returning from the Fourth Gulf War. "Eskander came in when he was just promoted to Nightpath, and we made a connection."

She wasn't lying. I had come in to meet her, several times, in my early days working for NIGHT. What she didn't mention is that every time I visited her, it was to inquire about certain revolutionary informants in the city that were outside of the purview of the Pacific South NIGHT headquarters on Alcatraz.

"What's a night bath?" Alex asked, stuffing the remains of a fried potato in his mouth.

"Three-nil!" my father jumped out of his seat at the edge of the couch, nearly dropping his forgotten lunch plate. Our seats buzzed faintly with the goal, and the player holograms ran across the vividly green pitch to celebrate with a section of fans that was closest to the field. For his part, my father clenched his fist victoriously, peering closely at the three-dimensional stadium with the gusto of a child appraising a freshly made sand castle.

My mother clucked at him irritably. "Sit *down*, Art," she said, ripping off a tiny piece of her sandwich and handing it down to the opening of the increasingly precarious-looking cushion fort. A tiny hand snatched it and retreated, Perinaz having made herself comfortable within.

"A Nightpath," my mother said, glancing testily again at my still-celebrating father, "is someone who protects humans from auric revolutionaries."

"Here we go," Suzan said sardonically, reaching for a handful of fried potatoes.

"I didn't *protect* them, mom," I said, feeling my blood pressure rise with the direction of the conversation. My parents also knew which buttons to push. "I gathered information about revolutionary movements to better serve interracial relations-"

"Bah!" my father said, sitting down and joining the conversation for the first time. "He was a patsy, telling tales on his own people for the good of the government. I'm glad he's working for the one true king, now."

"In *any* case," my mother continued speaking to Alex as if she hadn't been interrupted, "your uncle served as a secret agent for many years, until King Thog'run made him his spymaster."

"Chief of Intelligence, mom," I corrected.

"Who's Thog-a-run?" Perinaz's muffled voice carried through the walls of the pillow fort.

"King of Aurichome!" my father was an expert at carrying conversations while keeping his eyes glued to the ARTV. "Champion of the underraces and regent of San Francisco."

"What's an underrace?" Alex said thoughtfully. He had unconsciously scooted over on the loveseat and was now resting his head against Alina's arm.

"It's not a nice word, Lexi," Suzan said quickly, brushing her fingers with a napkin. "When people like your great-grandmother started living underground because they looked different, and had nowhere else to live, humans started calling aurics 'underraces.'"

It was a half-truth told to a child to keep him sheltered from real-world ironies. With the discovery of ceridium, a new stable and reproducible element that now powered over a third of the earth, the first generation of aurics began appearing in urban centers where ceridium was prevalent. It had unlocked a genetic mutation that had lain dormant for centuries, remembered only in myths about fantastic non-human creatures and the existence of a magical ingredient known as blue orichalcum.

In the twenty twenties, green researchers had struck gold – or, more accurately, blue – with what they called ceridium, an azure-hued synthetic version of blue orichalcum which could be manufactured, recycled, and importantly, monetized. It now powered everything that only fossil fuels once could, and most things that they could not, from flash-frying stoves and anti-gravity boostered cars to augmented reality digital ads and cerujets.

The return of ceridium saw a resurgence of schools of magic as well. Equipped with this missing component of spells, charms, curses, and worse, fringe groups began experimenting with ancient texts that had required the element to function. It wasn't long before unofficial institutions for the advancement of magical education began to crop up, which were in turn quickly quashed or regulated by the powers-that-be.

World governments weren't far behind. The

United States provided a model of paramilitary response to the rapidly expanding communities of ceridium-unlocked races and magic users with the National Intelligence Guard of Human Technology, or NIGHT. The public-facing mission of NIGHT, and national organizations like it, was to facilitate relations between humans and the new races, while enforcing the regulation of newly-discovered magics, including terramancy, pyromancy, and shadowmancy. It housed elite intelligence specialists such as Nightpaths, Daypaths, and Inquisitors, whose namesakes were drawn from their respective specializations as well as jurisdictions. In practice, the organization enforced the will of the government in a fashion that was much more surveillant than it was inclusive, which was not unfamiliar to the American populace.

The "underraces," as they were called, were treated on a spectrum that ranged from mild suspicion to open hostility. Human societies, raised on the xenophobia of red and green scare tactics from previous generations, were all too ready to turn their attention to a new common enemy. The new races were genetically identical to humans except for a tiny mutation that, when exposed to ceridium over an extended period of time, resulted in several different sets of phenotypic variation. Dwarves were, as expected, shorter and stouter than humans, with small and sometimes curling horns protruding from their foreheads. Trolls were considerably larger, with hulking frames and broad faces marred only by giant protruding noses and floppy ears. Gnomes were child-sized, bald, and for the most part genetically myopic. The rest of the underraces were recognizable only by a handful of observable features, whether they be the short tusks and flat noses of the so-called low aurics, or the almond-shaped eyes and curving, leaf-shaped ears of high aurics.

In some places, they were mocked, in others, persecuted. With the exception of a small minority of forward-thinking communities – specifically those which had themselves experienced some ongoing form of marginalization – the underraces were initially viewed as aberrations of humanity and not to be trusted. They lived a harried and harrowed existence on the fringes of society for nearly a generation, until public interest groups began to force the greater society to make space, literally and figuratively, for the rapidly growing underrace populace. Second generationers were gradually accepted into the general workforce and even public office, although old perceptions were very difficult to change. The duality of the "underrace" moniker held, as the new races largely lived underground in the crowded human metropolises, and were overall treated as second-class citizens.

It all changed with Thog'run II.

In an age of unprecedented surveillance and documentation, it was perhaps ironic that very little was publicly known about the auric king's childhood and early life. A first generationer born to a small farming family in central California, Thog'run had only showed up on government records as a teenager, beginning with his enlistment into the military. The armed forces comprised one of the first avenues of underrace participation in wider society, as it had been for minorities before them, and provided a venue for Thog'run's particular brand of strategic genius. He quickly made a name for himself as a lieutenant and then captain in the Third Gulf War, but became inevitably disillusioned with the ways in which underraces would give their lives for their countries, yet still endured second-class status when they returned home. Shortly after the war, he went to ground, disappearing once again from the books.

It's unclear whether Thog'run knew which way the wind was blowing, or if the wind itself marched to the tune of the imminent auric king, but when he resurfaced, there was hell to be paid. The Fourth Gulf War was in full swing when Thog'run's revolutionary forces commandeered a military base in the Marin Headlands of Northern California, with the name "Aurichome" on their lips. Caught with their pants down and their military elsewhere, the United States government and the NIGHTs quickly capitulated the region in a matter of days, allowing the revolutionaries to set about building their new capital a figurative stone's throw from the Pacific South NIGHT headquarters.

Thog'run immediately called the underraces from around the globe to ally with Aurichome, granting them sanctuary and even offering amnesty to human individuals and nations who recognized him as king. He gave the underraces a name: aurics, which was an interpretation of the historical term orichites, itself used to describe races affected by blue orichalcum in ages long before. Its root also shared the name with an ion of gold, suggesting the value of the aurics' worth, rather than the deficiency represented by the "underrace" moniker.

In the years that followed, Thog'run and his constituents had built Aurichome to a nation-state that rivaled most small countries in influence and military strength. A recent failed attempt by the NIGHT leadership in the form of William D. Karthax, the erstwhile Inquisitor General, to unseat Thog'run had resulted in Aurichome annexing San Francisco and the greater Bay Area. Karthax's treachery had been exposed, Thog'run gained official political recognition for Aurichome from the U.S. government and the NIGHTs, and I got a new job. It had been a long year of building and rebuilding since then.

"So are we underraces or aurics?" Alex was asking, drawing me out of my reverie.

"Both," Suzan replied smoothly, "but being called aurics is much *nicer*."

Alex nodded, satisfied with the response for now. He fidgeted with a button on his pants, still leaning against Alina.

"Alina," my mother began, changing the subject, "you should speak with Art about baseball! I'm sure you'll have a lot to talk about."

My father drew himself away from the soccer match for the briefest of moments, again looking at Alina as if in a new light.

"Hadzic?" he asked, recognition finally dawning in his almond-shaped eyes. "Relief pitcher for the Giants for the sixty-eight series?"

Alina touched her cap in recognition. "It was a tough one, but we ground it out."

My father looked from Alina to me, approval written all over his face. "Impressive," he said.

I blushed uncharacteristically.

"Actually," Alina said, putting her arm around Alex comfortably, "the reason I came by was to remind Eskander about an upcoming charity event sponsored by Aurichome. The king is sponsoring a Veterans' All-Star game this weekend, and I'll be pitching an inning or so to represent the National League West."

I nodded, remembering the details without needing to look at my digitab's calendar. "I'll be there, Alina."

"I want to go!" Perinaz's voice piped from within the pillow fort.

"Me too!" Alex said, snuggling closer to Alina on the loveseat.

"Well," Alina said, looking at me for endorsement, if not consent, "I'm sure we could easily get tickets for all of you, if you'd like to come."

I shrugged, resigned. It would be a mess trying to wrangle my family at what would ordinarily be a work event for me, but I couldn't see a way out of it.

"Sure," I said.

"Yay!" the children yelled in unison. My father grinned at the prospect of going to a live sports game, particularly one in which he now personally knew one of the players.

"It's a date!" my mother said, beaming.

TWO

He has betrayed not a person, nor only a people. He has betrayed an idea, that there is such a thing as birthright, that there is such a place as homeland, that there is such a truth as justice. He destroys nothing, betrays no one, more than himself.

-Thog'run II, King of Aurichome

To say that the rest of the week passed eventfully would be an understatement. I've learned the hard way that the whims of my family can be as capricious as they come, and have long resigned myself to having very little going according to plan while they visit. In the days leading up to Alina's charity game, I counted no less than three trips to the Wal-Amazon Center, a giant multilevel shopping arena in Daly City, south of San Francisco. Getting in and out of the Center was a traffic nightmare, but Alex or Perinaz would inevitably lose a shoe or need a new toy, and my family was keen to get out of my small apartment, for which I didn't begrudge them. I was asked more than once about my relationship with

Alina, and wasn't relishing any further awkwardness by seeing her in a public setting.

Coordinating an outing to the mall or multiplex required no small amount of effort, but trying to wrangle the whole family to get to an event on time was an entirely different endeavor. We had to wait until the Giants, who were playing away in Chicago, finished their game so that my father wouldn't have to watch it on the ARTV in their rental van, which made him motion sick. We were dangerously close to being on time, and had to return to my apartment twice to pick up a pair of shorts for Perinaz, who was warm, and a bag of freeze-dried banana chips for Alex, who was hungry.

It was difficult to imagine what getting to a baseball game in San Francisco must have been like in the years before antigravity boostered vehicles. As it stood, we sat in thirty minutes of upper level traffic traversing the two crowded city miles between my apartment and the stadium. Non-boostered merging cars languished in the gridlock below us, fighting for supremacy in the weekend rush. My family's rental van was serviceable if not fancy, and glided silently through the city streets with a ceridium-powered engine that must have been built in the previous decade.

The delays from my sister's children and traffic meant that the beginning of the game started without us, so we all followed along with the ARTV in the center console of the vehicle. The audio from the van's outdated multi-speakers blocked out Perinaz and Alex's quarreling in the very rear of the vehicle, although I could see in my rearview mirror

Suzan and my mother turning in their middle seats in an attempt to mollify them. My father alternated between glancing at the action on the holodisplay between us, and sticking his head out the window in the hopes that the fresh air would ameliorate his queasiness.

The world had changed irreversibly with the introduction of ceridium and its subsequent revelation of forgotten races and magics, but some things were eternal. Baseball was among the latter.

Sports had always provided a sense of the familiar during times of political turmoil, and the unrest posed by the introduction of the first underraces in the twenty twenties presented an ideal opportunity for strengthening civic tribalism. Nations at war with themselves over the citizenship status of the new races were all too happy to pledge their allegiances to local teams that fit the overarching narratives of *us* versus *them*, even as ticket prices broke more records than did athletes, and teams became franchised to an extreme state of corporatization.

Incredibly, the constant civil wars that wreaked havoc on the Middle East pushed the globalization of previously single-nation sports to a new level. After the discovery of ceridium, western powers slowly attempted to remove their oil-stained fingers from the area, and found that their interests were still too entrenched to support the surreptitious exit they had intended. The Third and Fourth Gulf Wars were fought over the course of decades, on the initial pretense of protecting strategic territories from the uprisings that took place as larger communities of underraces struggled to establish themselves. Unspoken was the undercurrent of war for war's sake, the ghosts of history rearing their heads in a region that no longer held any interest in reconciliation.

Sports, however, leveraged the seemingly contradictory aspects of the human psyche that found comfort simultaneously in globalization and xenophobia. Governments and people – the U.S. foremost among them – enjoyed participating on a global stage, if only to prove to themselves that they were better than their neighbors. The self-proclaimed World Series, for example, which had paradoxically only included baseball teams from the U.S. and Canada, provided the groundwork for the first quadrennial Global Series in the thirties. The Global Series took a page from the World Cup, Olympics, and similar sporting events and invited over thirty countries to take part in a three-week festival every four years, and had named champions from six different nations since its inception. It, along with other global competitions, served as a lightning rod for public nationalism that could be peaceful in times of war, fraught as it was with its own brand of politics and institutionalized racism.

Alina Hadzic, my sort-of girlfriend, was a prime example of how politics and baseball could come together for better, and undeniably for worse. As a player, she was the consummate relief pitcher, with a nasty curveball that could leave even the most aggressive power hitter looking. The first half-auric woman to play in the majors, she exploded onto the scene with a no-hitter in the

2062 World Series, followed by another championship and three record-breaking appearances in the global competition. The sport had rarely seen an athlete with her unique brand of raw skill and unflappable confidence in the face of high-pressure moments. In my very biased mind, she was the best pitcher of her generation of players.

Everything changed for her with the Fourth Gulf War.

In what seemed to many among her peers as being an impulsive and racially motivated decision, Alina enlisted in the military to, as she explained in a press conference after her retirement game, serve her country's interests instead of her own. She was deployed within a year, and what she saw and experienced while there changed her, and not for the better.

Alina had always been a savvy player in the media, and quick to downplay her minority status as an auric female in a predominantly human male game, but upon her return, she became extremely vocal about the second-class citizenship of the underraces, along with the U.S. government's inability to ameliorate their condition and NIGHT's continued exacerbation of the issue. Her hard-won celebrity platform deteriorated as her newfound alignment with Aurichome became apparent, and she settled into relative anonymity as the owner of an underrace-friendly sports bar, *They Might Be Giant*, in the Richmond district of San Francisco.

Among her own, however, the aurics still knew her as their Pitcher. She had traded fame for dedication to a cause in which she believed, and was rewarded, through events that had transpired a year ago, by becoming King Thog'run's hand-picked Consul for Human-Auric Relations. *They Might Be Giant* was no more, having been destroyed by the blast of an entromancer's incantation, but Alina still had her curveball, and a battery of terramancer spells from her time as a soldier.

It had only been a year since Aurichome had annexed San Francisco, but Thog'run's memory was long, and his court had immediately begun planning events to leverage what relationships existed between the underrace nation and the city that housed the Pacific South NIGHT headquarters, the seat of NIGHT power in California. The Golden Gate Bridge, which had stood dark and solemn for many years, had reopened to much fanfare after the deposition of the corrupt NIGHT Inquisitor General, William D. Karthax, last year, and friendly sporting events that brought auric and human athletes together in competition were almost painfully obvious in their attempt to demonstrate unity.

Today's game was one such event, pitting veteran stars of the National League against those from the American League in typical baseball fashion. It would be Alina's first pitching engagement since her retirement game, and I was unsure of how she would be received by the teams and their spectators. There was no love lost between herself and her erstwhile fan base, but with Aurichome on the rise, it was indeed a brave new world.

We arrived, parked, and made our way interminably to our seats after spending half an hour or more purchasing so many hot dogs, sodas, and popcorn that it would appear to an onlooker as though none of us had eaten for a week. When we finally sat down in our row, about halfway up from the field and facing third base, we had missed the first four innings and were forced to wait for a pitching change.

It was a beautiful day for baseball. The 1:05PM start time for the charity game ensured that Aurikar Park, as the stadium had been renamed, would benefit from the last warm rays of a Bay Area summer sun that refused to concede to autumn without a fight. The ballpark smelled like grass and peanuts, and the air was heavy enough that if one was romantic about such things, one could imagine the scent of pine bats and oiled leather gloves on the warm wind that capriciously graced the one hundred and twenty thousand spectator seats. Small drones flitted about the park, recording the action from innumerable angles or delivering concessions to fans in their seats.

To our right, on the second level of the park behind home plate and below the press box, sat a very motley array of dignitaries, security guards, and officials from NIGHT and Aurichome. I easily spotted Marguerite Liu, or Madge, as I knew her, NIGHT's newest Inquisitor General, flanked by Striker Johnson, my former dispatcher and Madge's personal security, and another Inquisitor whom I couldn't recognize from this distance. Striker's cybernetic arm and breastplate glinted menacingly in the midday sun, the Nightpath having chosen to keep them exposed intimidatingly by donning a simple combat vest and fatigues. A handful of other NIGHT agents and personnel sat placidly in their section.

To their left sat King Thog'run and his court, unmistakable in their archaic blue and white livery that was emblazoned with the seal of Aurichome. Two small pennants framed the king's seat, dwarfed by his incredible stature that, even while seated, was frightening. Every now and then, the broadcast feed would cut to a shot of him and Madge as if to demonstrate their shared enjoyment in the event as a show of solidarity, but while Madge was animated about the game, Thog'run was implacable. His beady black eyes were cold and hard, even on the ARTV, and his monstrous visage was only reinforced by the yellow tusks that protruded under his pronounced porcine snout. His signature topknot was braided, as if for battle, and he sat with the erect posture of a soldier, rarely turning to one side or the other to give the appearance of making conversation with Madge or one of his own lieutenants.

Next to him was Fazgha Hezdottr, Queen of Aurichome and a devastating low auric terramancer in her own right. Several rows behind them sat their firstborn, Thog'run III, amidst a host of other family members, security, and emissaries. None of them looked comfortable, except for Vasshka "Doubleshot" Lestrage, a revolutionary who had been in service to the crown for longer than I can remember. The dwarf sat a short ways from the crown prince with her booted feet propped up on a railing, somehow drawing from a cigar in a stadium that had long ago prohibited smoking. A wide-brimmed black hat shaded her face from the sunlight, undoubtedly blocking the view of the person seated behind her.

I snickered, feeling a little weird about not being seated among the Aurichome contingent, given my status as Chief of Intelligence, but it was just as well. Given the clown show that my family's current visit had proven to be, I was happy to not allow their admittedly well-meaning shenanigans spill over into my work life.

Our section, although featuring an incredible view of the pitcher's mound and the general action, was more functional than ostentatious, with simple plastic seats and cupholders and palm-sized AR displays stationed between every other seat back that piped in the live broadcast feed. You could sync a digitab to it to hear the announcers calling the action while it happened, but as a purist, I settled in with a comfortable sigh to watch the game the old-fashioned way.

"I'm bored!" Perinaz said imperiously, her little feet not quite touching the cement floor below her seat.

"Be patient, Naz," Suzan admonished, gently bouncing a sleeping Memet in a reinforced cloth wrap that clung to her chest. "Alina will be up to pitch soon. Won't that be exciting?"

Perinaz looked dubious, but managed to sit quietly while my mother doused her and Alex with sunscreen.

It took a couple of scoreless innings, which my father and I watch with rapt attention and the rest of the family tolerated, until Alina was called up to the mound. She strode up from the bullpen with the confidence of a bullfighter, dressed in the orange and white uniform of her home team, the Giants, her name and number emblazoned on the back of her jersey. To my extreme delight, she was greeted with a raucous ovation from both the aurikar contingent and the stadium at large, and acknowledged the crowd with a simple touch of her cap.

As a right-hander, her body turned in our direction as she took the mound, her feet pointing towards third base as she stared at the catcher behind home plate for her quick warm-up. She had been called into a two-on, no-out situation, which, my father attempted to explain to anyone who would listen, meant that the previous pitcher had allowed a runner each to reach second and third base, without having successfully struck out any batters.

In a regular season game, it would have been a high-pressure situation, given that the relief pitcher would have had very little room for error. The game was tied at 2-2, and if Alina gave up a single, the American League team would likely score to go ahead, and it was late enough in the game that such a thing could spell victory.

This being a charity event, with nothing riding on it except pride, the pressure on Alina was more imagined than real, it being her first public appearance after her retirement game and everything that ensued after her deployment. The game, I knew, and what it represented, meant more to her personally than to anyone else on the field.

Yet, if the Pitcher felt any nervousness, none of it showed as she completed her warmup, leaning down to grab the chalk bag at her feet to dust her fingers with it as the next batter walked up to the plate.

Alina set up for her first pitch, her right foot just barely touching the rubber strip at the apex of the mound. The ballpark, ordinarily filled with ambient chatter, home team chants, and the incessant hum of concession drones, seemed to hush, having unknowingly been waiting for this moment for a decade or more. The Pitcher stared emotionlessly at the catcher across from her, shaking off the first call that he proposed, then nodding at the second. She looked down briefly, as was her habit, then wound up, lifting her left knee to her chest and turning her hips to release the baseball from the tip of her right hand with a grunt.

The pitch crossed the distance in a flash, disappearing into the catcher's meaty glove with a thud. Fastball, ninety-four miles-per-hour, just a little inside. It was a mean, challenging first pitch, and the batter watched it cross over the plate for a strike.

Some small applause resounded around the ballpark with appreciation for Alina's daring and accuracy, particularly after so many years away from the game.

"Fast pitch," my father said appraisingly. I nodded.

Alina set up again, turning her head from home plate to second base and back again to check on the two runners at second and third, although they had nowhere to go, even if they were to decide to steal. She again shook off the catcher's first two suggestions, being satisfied with the third.

She wound up and released with another grunt. The nasty curveball, her signature pitch, made its way from top to bottom of the strike zone, again to nestle safely in the catcher's mitt. The batter swung for power, too early, and almost spun around with the force of his missed swing. Strike two.

"Is that Alina?" Alex asked belatedly.

"Yes, Alex," my mother said, shushing him.

Alina pitched the curveball again, a little lower, and the batter didn't bite, earning a ball. The catcher threw the baseball back to her, and, after checking the base runners, Alina set up for another pitch.

I looked over to Madge and Thog'run's section, which was rapt, along with the rest of the stadium. Even the king seemed to be more at attention than usual, if such a thing were possible, and Doubleshot had sat up straight, which was saying a lot for her.

Alina released her pitch, another fastball, inside, ninety-six miles-per-hour. It was almost exactly the same pitch as her first.

The batter took the bait, swinging for the fences, but was too slow, striking out. A bit more applause greeted the Pitcher as the opposing team player walked back to the dugout, and Alina stoically received the baseball from the catcher and set up for the next player.

"She's really good," my father offered, and I couldn't agree more. I had seen her in battle action with a magically-enhanced ceridium orb that Gloric Vunderfel, our friend and Thog'run's Chief of Technology, had created for her, but somehow watching the mundane version was more authentic and inspiring.

The second batter fared similarly to the first, with Alina striking out the left-handed hitter with a cunningly placed cutter that moved towards his hands as it tore across the plate. The crowd began to start voicing its support, applauding each of her well-placed strikes and groaning in dismay when a ball was called in favor of the opposing team.

The third at-bat was a battle, the batter reading Alina's pitches well and foul-tipping a few to stay alive, building up to a 3-2 count. The catcher took a moment to walk up to the pitcher's mound, covering his mouth with his glove as he and Alina talked over a potential strategy.

"See, they have three balls, and two strikes," my father explained, pointing up at the gigantic scoreboard to our left that displayed game and player statistics. "If she throws another ball, he gets to walk to first base."

"I know how baseball works, dad," Suzan said, dexterously opening a bag of chips for Perinaz with one hand as she supported Memet's bundle against her chest with the other.

"I was telling your mom," my father retorted.

"I *know* what a walk is, Art," my mother admonished.

My father gave me a helpless look, and I just shrugged.

Alina set up again, checking on the runners, and settling in to pitch. She threw a filthy, oily hanging curveball, almost a slider, that somehow managed to move from outside of the strike zone to drop right over the plate into the catcher's waiting glove, which he brought up to center to frame the pitch and sway the opinion of the umpire squatting behind him that the ball was hittable.

The umpire stood unceremoniously, calling it a ball.

The crowd erupted in boos and catcalls as the batter tossed his bat to the side and trotted up to first base, creating an even higher-pressured situation based on what the stadium at large – or, at least, the National League and home fans – thought was a bad call.

"Why are they booing?" Perinaz asked, genuinely interested, although most likely because it was Alina pitching rather than due to any real enthusiasm for the game. My sister's children had taken to soccer at a very young age, but the intricacies of baseball still eluded them.

"It was a good pitch, but a better take," I said, as though that explained everything.

"What's a 'take?'" Alex queried, his mouth full of popcorn.

"It's when you don't swing at a pitch," Suzan said before my father could answer.

"What's a pitch?" Alex asked.

"When you throw the *ball*," Perinaz said admonishingly, grabbing her seat arms and turning towards her brother, as though he had forgotten his own name and was asking the group to remind him.

The fourth batter walked up to the plate, a burly right-handed human woman whose name escaped me, but who had played in the majors and served in the military around the same time as Alina. She was known for being a power hitter, having set the record for the most home runs in a single season by a female player. She scuffed her shoes on the dirt next to home plate, making a little divot for her to stand in, and touching her helmet superstitiously before gripping the bat with two hands, awaiting the first pitch.

Alina stared ahead, her eyes barely visible under the brim of her baseball cap, the warm wind briefly setting her pony tail fluttering behind her. Three runners stood at her back and sides with the bases loaded, the game suddenly pregnant with excitement and anticipatory energy.

The Pitcher looked down, then up, moving through her windup and release. Fastball, ninety-eight miles-per-hour, right down the throat of home plate. It was as bold of a challenge as a pitcher could muster, and she threw it perfectly.

The batter, to her credit, would not be outdone, and she swung, with a severe, graceless chop that would have felled a redwood tree. She caught the tail of the pitch, sending the ball careening into the spectator seats, foul.

Pitcher, batter, and catcher reset, along with the rest of the field players and runners, who had moved away from their bases to lead off in case of a hit. The crowd seemed to take a moment as well, having held its collective breath for the beginning of this matchup.

The second pitch came, almost the same as the first, but off-speed, ninety-two miles-per-hour, to throw off the batter's timing. The batter swung, missing it completely. Strike two.

The crowd began to pick up momentum, smelling blood. One by one, sections began to stand, cheering incoherently or chanting Alina's name, willing her to strike out the batter to end

the inning. The call of "Had-*zic*! Had-*zic*!"
became a percussive litany that filled the
stadium, and to me at least, felt symbolic of
something that I couldn't discern in the
excitement of the moment.

I found myself standing among them, my
parents and sister doing the same, with Suzan
encouraging the kids to stand on their chairs so
they could see over the crowd in front of us.

"Had-*zic*!" I said, almost compulsively. It was
difficult not to get swept up in the excitement.

Alina threw her next pitch with a grunt, her
curveball, hoping that she had worked up the
batter with the previous two pitches and would
get her to bite. The catcher collected the
baseball just outside of the strike zone, and the
batter took it, not swinging. Ball one.

The crowd, myself among them, exhaled,
waiting for the players to reset their positions
before taking up our chant anew, and with
more force and bluster. Even Perinaz and Alex
stood attentively, Alex on his tiptoes,
enraptured by the game of chess between
Pitcher, batter, and catcher.

Alina stared, emotionless, callous, hard, at
the catcher, flicking her head to the side curtly
to shake off the first three pitches he suggested.
With two strikes and one ball, she had some
room to not throw a strike, but she clearly had
no interest in anything but. The Pitcher wanted
to end this, as efficiently as possible.

She set up, looking from second base back to
home plate, her right hand curled around the
baseball in the protective leather of her left
hand glove, two small drones hovering twenty
feet above her to capture every bit of the

Pitcher's movement in detail. Alina wound up, her body coiling like a spring, the stadium thrumming with power and deafening with the roar of her name.

Out of the corner of my eye, far to the right, I noticed a sudden movement in Madge and Thog'run's section behind home plate.

Alina released her pitch, the grunt of her effort lost in the din of the crowd.

The batter swung, connecting with the ball with a crack, her bat breaking in the process.

The stadium held its breath, its abrupt silence creating a vacuum in the late summer air.

The ball rocketed over the infield, Alina and the rest of the ballpark turning to mark its trajectory as the base runners began their movement.

Time stopped.

A cry pealed from the section behind home plate.

Pandemonium erupted.

I heard, rather than saw, one of the outfield players catch the fly ball as it made its way to – but not past – the dirt warning track that encircled the field, my attention drawn to the commotion in the dignitary section. The people around me, my family included, were jumping up and down, cheering, as Alina completed her shutout inning with a stunning display of skill and ferocity, but I saw none of it, my eyes fixed on the unfolding scene.

A group of thirty or more spectators, dressed in ordinary civilian clothing, was battling its way through the guards that surrounded the aurikar and NIGHT contingents, who seemed utterly unprepared for an attack. Thog'run's revolutionaries and Madge's NIGHT agents, with few exceptions, were struggling to unholster their weapons as they were accosted by fans that surrounded their section.

In the midst of everyone was the most physically imposing man I have ever seen, an enormous human with curly black hair flowing behind him and muddy green tattoos covering his bronzed skin. He yelled as he cut a path through the aurikar and NIGHT guards, wielding an incomparably huge greatsword with two hands. Both he and the sword sparkled with an eerie blue light that stood out brightly against the carnage that trailed in his path.

"Get away," I said, moving in the direction of the commotion. No one could hear me in the excitement of the game, and I pushed past Suzan roughly enough that she jumped back, startled.

"What's going on, Eskander?" she exclaimed, clutching Memet protectively.

"I said get *away*," I yelled, taking half a second to look back at her, reaching for the off-duty ceridium pistol hidden at my hip.

What she saw in my eyes, I couldn't be sure. But it scared her, and I felt a twinge of emotion that shamed me. I softened my expression.

"Go, take them," I pleaded, waving towards the rest of the family, who began to look up from the game. "This isn't good," I added.

"Eskander?" I heard my mother saying to my back as I drew the pistol, cursing myself for leaving my nightblade at home.

"Where's he going?" my father asked.

"We've got to go," my sister said, her voice

turning to iron as I jumped onto the arm of a chair, trying to make it around the startled fans to the nearest aisle. I silently thanked her for not questioning me and trying to get our family out of harm's way.

By the time I had picked my way to the aisle, the crowd had settled from the initial excitement of the flyout, and was slowly turning its attention in confusion to the melee behind home plate. Even Alina, I saw from one of the AR broadcasts, was turning in consternation towards the activity, her hand still lifting her cap to the fans in appreciation for their support.

Without hesitation, I grabbed a ceridium capsule from my pocket and crushed it, muttering the words to an incantation as I leapt from a plastic seat back into the air. The shadowmancy spell opened a gaping black portal in front of me, transporting me just over a hundred feet to the next section, where I hit the ground running.

I wasn't close enough to do any damage, and had to repeat the spell, crushing another capsule to power my jump through the shadow ether, reappearing past groups of onlookers that were beginning to panic and heading for the exits.

It took me an excruciating amount of time to reach the struggle, made more difficult by the sheer amount of people in my path. The would-be-assassins were in full assault on the aurikar and NIGHT forces by the time I arrived, the giant making his way ever closer to the center of the section, where a number of guards were attempting to usher a reluctant Madge and Thog'run away from the action and into the relative safety of the spectator tunnels that led away from the seating.

Not having a clear shot at anyone near the royal party, I focused my attention on the giant, who painted a huge target. Sighting down the pistol, I fired a silent ceridium bullet towards his sizeable torso, only to see it harmlessly dissipate into the blue glow that surrounded him.

I didn't have time to consider the situation as an assassin to my right removed his blade from the neck of an aurikar guard and swung it with precision at my face. Cursing myself again for not equipping my nightblade, I caught his wrist with my free hand, smashing the butt of my pistol into his face. A muffled cry escaped his broken lips as I ducked under his arm, using the force of the motion to bring his body downwards as I swept his feet out from under him with my trailing leg. He fell to the concrete, unconscious.

I ran down the row of seats, jumping over assassin and guard bodies, finally reaching the heart of the fray. Striker was shouting instructions at the NIGHT agents embroiled in protecting the dignitary group from the assailants, his large metal frame interposed between the retreating NIGHT and Aurichome leadership. Aurikar soldiers fought alongside Nightpaths and Daypaths, their blades and spells making quick work of the would-be assassins now that the elite warriors and agents had recovered from the initial attack.

None of them fought as ferociously as the giant, who, from this close distance, could be heard chanting a battle cry of some sort, in a language that sounded tribal and unfamiliar to me. It was melodic, percussive, and terrible. Suffused with power, the spellsong lifted and fell with every chop of his greatsword, which was swung with deadly accuracy. He made his way ever closer to the retreating royal party, and although I was confident in their own ability to protect themselves, his was a magic for which I knew they would be wholly unprepared.

I had to stop him.

Doubleshot appeared to my right, her twin ceridium pistols smoking with blue light and her wide-brimmed hat somehow still stuck to her head. Errant trails of fiery orange hair peaked out from within, the only signs that the dwarf had seen battle action.

"I'll try to get his attention from the flank," she said gruffly.

I nodded, gauging the distance, and crushing my last ceridium capsule to shadow step into melee with the giant.

I stepped out of the shadows into his path just as he grabbed a NIGHT agent's face with his thick, hairy hand, tossing her into the seats below like a ragdoll. He looked up at me, startled, but continued his haunting song, lifting the greatsword over his head to strike.

Now, in front of him, and in peril, I was able to take his measure more clearly, and was unhappy with the result. He was nearly seven feet tall, and as wide around as a troll, his mouth foaming with saliva as the magical words of power escaped from his lips. His eyes were wide and bloodshot, as though in frenzy, but there was a cunning within them that frightened me. Tearstains marked his dark complexion and ran down a thick black beard, and there was a timbre to his voice that cut to my core, almost buckling my legs with emotion, right under the swing of his glowing sword.

He was weeping.

With nowhere to go in the skinny row of seats, I dashed forwards, under his chop, driving the blade of my free hand into his exposed throat, hoping that it would be a soft spot on his muscular body. The strike connected, and he choked for a split second, his song faltering. The protective glow that surrounded him flashed, and Vasshka took the opportunity to fire her pistols at him from behind, which caused him to roar in pain.

The giant recovered quickly, swatting at me with a hairy paw. I had run out of room, and he hit me squarely in the face, tossing me unceremoniously over the chairs to my right. I attempted desperately to twist my body into a roll, but landed painfully on a plastic chair back, knocking the wind out of myself.

I heard Striker's voice yelling obscenities, and the blaring of drone loudspeakers as they instructed stadium security to continue to escort audience members out of the building. I forced myself to sit up, scurrying gracelessly over the plastic chairs as I tried to follow the giant, who had reached the mouth of the tunnel through which Madge, Thog'run, and the others were escaping.

Then, as suddenly as it had begun, the melee ended. Inexplicably, as though on cue, the giant and the remaining assassins dropped their weapons, surrendering. The giant fell to his knees, dropping his greatsword to the floor with a clatter. NIGHT agents moved quickly to restrain him, while aurikar guards knocked out the other assassins.

I hobbled over to the mouth of the tunnel, dumbfoundedly holstering my pistol, which I had somehow kept holding in my failed attempt at a tumble. Doubleshot met me there, her pistols already put away, and lit a cigar.

"That went well," she said, disgusted.

I looked from her to the giant, who had stopped singing, and was providing no resistance as the agents bound him roughly in manacles. Even on his knees, he was almost as tall as I was.

Tears streamed down his face as he glanced up at me, the corners of his mouth flecked with spittle.

"What the hell was that?" I shouted at him, not knowing what else to say.

He looked at me in resignation, emotions twisting his face into a mask of rage and despair.

"Where is he?" a familiar voice boomed behind me, and I turned to see King Thog'run sweeping down the tunnel towards us, his blue and white cloak streaming behind him. He used his imposing frame to push aside a number of guards, including Striker, who were attempting to keep him away from harm.

He was a lion, and they were cattle. The auric king walked towards us with the aura of an animal unleashed, his snout quivering and eyes promising death. I had to remind myself that he was on our side, but even that was not very comforting.

"*WHERE IS HE?*" Thog'run shouted, leveling his fury at the giant, who, to his credit, was cowed by the king's fury.

The king looked down at him, anger etched through every wrinkle on his face, along with pain and something else.

"Where is my son?" he asked, low and threatening.

The giant let out a long, plaintive wail, rumbling and awful. "I'm sorry," he said simply.

THREE

The network itself is not magic; it is human made and machine propagated. Its method of propagation, however, is indeed magic.

-The Sigil of Sparks

"Thirty-seven-point-seven-nine by minus one-hundred-twenty-two-point-four-six" Gloric Vunderfel was saying, rattling off the latitudinal and longitudinal coordinates from his personal display. "Not far from the swamp."

The gnome was perched on a small platform close to Thog'run's throne in the king's audience chamber, his ebony fingers tapping away at a keyboard strapped to his portly waist. Tiny wisps of white hair trailed from underneath an unfashionable newsboy cap, and a single-eye display jutted in front of his oversized glasses, giving him more the appearance of a jeweler appraising a diamond rather than the king's Chief of Technology.

"That's what my latest ping from one of the assailants' digitab indicates, at least," he added, unconsciously adjusting the rounded Canterbury cross at the hollow of his throat. "They've taken the crown prince into the

Presidio."

Thog'run's eyes narrowed at that, and it was the first flicker of emotion from the king since we had returned to his sanctuary in Aurichome, roughly forty miles north of San Francisco proper. He had been dangerously quiet during Gloric's assessment of the situation and my own sitrep as Chief of Intelligence.

It had not gone well. Thog'run's audience chamber, austere as it was with its marble floor and concrete walls, was ordinarily a hushed place of reverence and power. Thick blue and white carpets and matching curtains attempted to soften the auditorium's atmosphere, and would have succeeded somewhat, if not for the severe augmented reality depictions of the royal family that stared down accusingly from intervals throughout the cavernous room. Large chandeliers provided a warm light that was stark against the AR holograms, some of which displayed grisly scenes of battle that reminded the viewer of the savagery committed in the building of a nation.

Since before we had arrived from Alina's abandoned baseball game, the audience chamber had devolved into a cacophony of officials, guards, and other functionaries racing back and forth between the sanctuary and their offices or communicating loudly through their digitabs. The attack on the royal party and subsequent abduction of the crown prince had thrown the king's court into complete disarray, and answers were sought after to forestall Thog'run II's inevitable ire. That a heavily armed force, posing as baseball fans, could organize an assault on the royal family, with dozens of aurikar and NIGHT guards present and stadium security besides, was an unthinkable, and very public, display of the vulnerability of both forces. From a security standpoint, it was a catastrophe.

The king had sat placidly on his marble and sandstone throne, his hand resting customarily on the head of his great battleaxe, listening to report after report without a hint of emotion. His staff, included me, were to a person on edge, waiting for Thog'run's imminent explosion of anger at our ineptitude, which hadn't yet come to pass. Gloric alone seemed unfazed, having been the only one to provide any semblance of information about the whereabouts of the crown prince.

As his Chief of Intelligence, or "spymaster," as the king liked to call me, the blame would ordinarily be squarely upon my shoulders for all of us having been caught with our pants down at the charity event, had I not been on approved holiday for the preceding two weeks. I was hoping against hope that my absence during the lead-up was worth something in the king's mind before he lashed out at someone, particularly because the assault had to have been months in the making, long before my vacation. If Thog'run turned his ire towards me, I wouldn't have much of a case on which to stand.

"Why the Presidio, Glory?" Alina asked, standing next to Gloric's platform with her arms folded. She had quickly changed out of her baseball uniform for a more serviceable getup of reinforced dark leather armor, a pouch containing her magical ceridium orb of returning at her hip. Her wolf companion, Buster, sat at her feet, happily panting in the underground air.

The technomancer shrugged. "They must have a safehouse in there that we don't know about," he said.

"And it'll be tough to get to," Tribe Achebe, the king's adoptive high auric nephew, offered from next to Thog'run's throne. The thief, now a vanguard in Aurichome's security forces, looked more punk than prince with his studded leather jacket, spiked hair, and myriad piercings and tattoos, with daggers displayed menacingly upon either hip.

I nodded. The Presidio had long been lost to monsters and worse, being a black hole to aurikar and NIGHT surveillance. If one was brave or foolish enough to seek refuge in the erstwhile military park, they could disappear from the network indefinitely.

"Your Highness, if I might offer," a voice lifted smoothly from the stairs that curved up to the king's dais from the audience chamber below. It belonged to a NIGHT Inquisitor, the woman I had seen in attendance with Madge's group at the baseball game. "My agents have interrogated the prisoner on NIGHT's behalf, and he has some interesting...information to share."

She sauntered up the stairs to our platform with a lithe grace that was almost sensual, her long brown hair gently bouncing with every step. Her formal, red-and-black Inquisitor's robes somehow contoured to her shapely form. She walked with authority, her eyes beaming warmth and inviting attention from all who could see her.

I noticed motion out of the corner of my eye and glanced at Alina, who was staring daggers at me, having caught my lingering glance on the advancing woman. I shrugged sheepishly.

The crowd of functionaries near us hushed as the Inquisitor glided to face Thog'run, his expression unreadable as she approached. The human bowed modestly, showing her knowledge of the court and deference to the king in his seat of power.

"What is your name, Inquisitor?" the queen, Fazgha Hezdottr, said from next to Thog'run's throne, her blond hair draped over each shoulder in thick, tight braids and yellow tusks jutting diagonally across her lips. If she was concerned about the whereabouts of the crown prince, she showed no more emotion about it than did the king.

"Damara Drivas, your grace," the woman said, inclining her head politely in the queen's direction. "Special advisor to Marguerite Liu, Inquisitor General of the National Intelligence Guard of Human Technology."

"I'm pretty sure the queen knows who NIGHT is," Vasshka said under her breath, next to me. The dwarf stuck a thick finger in her mouth rudely, picking at something between her teeth.

"If you'll allow us," Damara continued, turning her attention to the king, "we'll bring the auromancer up for questioning...in private, of course," she added.

All eyes turned to Thog'run, who sat quietly on his stone throne, one hand still gripping the head of his giant battleaxe. At length, he waved his free hand, no more than a flick, indicating his approval.

At once, a dozen or more officials and functionaries gathered themselves and filtered out of the audience chamber, leaving a handful of Thog'run's elite warriors and our little group standing on the dais. After some time, two aurikar guards dragged a very battered and bruised giant into the room and up one of the side staircases, their arms bulging with the effort of carrying his weight.

The guards dropped him in a heap in front of the king, Damara sliding across the dais to make room for his hulking form. The giant was breathing heavily, his curly black hair and beard matted with blood and his brown face ugly with bruises.

Slowly, like a bear emerging from its winter cave, Thog'run stood from his throne, carefully, almost lovingly, leaning his axe to the side of it. He stalked towards the giant, his heavy boots thudding loudly even on the thick carpets.

"Andrew Alyawarre," Damara's voice echoed from the side of the dais. "An aboriginal auromancer of minor repute from Brisbane, Australia."

Auromancer? Alina mouthed at me from across the dais. I shrugged, not understanding the word either. Gloric, still perched near the throne, was typing furiously on his little portable keyboard, reading something on his lens display.

Thog'run looked at the big man, unreadable. The giant raised his bloodied head, feeling danger to be imminent.

"Please," he said, his voice cracking.

The king stared down at him impassively,

light from the room's chandeliers flashing on his metal armor as his fist connected with the giant's jaw with a crack. The thunderous blow flattened the man to the ground with the force of a battering ram, teeth and blood splattering the pristine carpet. He slumped awkwardly, unmoving.

"Heal him," Thog'run said simply.

The queen shuffled over to the giant, the fire in her eyes the only sign of her anger.   She drew a mortar and pestle from within her terramancer's robes, followed by a handful of unidentifiable herbs intermixed with the unmistakable azure glow of ceridium powder. Crushing the mixture with the pestle, she spoke several words of power, the blue glow spilling over the mortar and encompassing the human's limp form at her feet.

The giant began to rouse as the queen's spell took effect, closing his wounds and restoring his body to normal. I caught Alina's eye across from me, quirking an eyebrow, and she nodded appraisingly, impressed.

The auromancer made an attempt at raising himself to one knee, at which point Thog'run kicked him in the midsection with a heavy boot, sprawling the giant onto his back. Fazgha's spell continued, healing the giant almost instantaneously while the king did his work.

It went on for several squeamish minutes, most of us either looking away or exchanging uncomfortable glances with one another as Thog'run took the giant apart, only to have him put back together by the queen. It was a fascinating, macabre display of their combined power, and it appeared to be a practice that they were familiar with employing. I shuddered, thinking about the fates of others who had crossed the king – most notably, an entromancer that I had helped put behind Aurichome bars only a year prior.

Finally, Thog'run grabbed the giant by the jaw, the king's own hand covered in the man's blood. Though the human was at least a foot taller than the low auric king, Thog'run lifted him with ease, holding him several inches off the ground.

"Who sent you?" the king growled from between gritted teeth.

"I don't know," the giant coughed, wounds on his body knitting themselves together as the queen's spell continued.

The king punched him in the stomach with his free hand.

"Answer differently!" he shouted angrily. I tore my eyes away to look at Tribe, who had been estranged from the royal family until the events of last year had brought him back into the fold. His olive, normally jovial face was pinched in disgust, clearly not enjoying the scene.

"I don't know," the auromancer repeated, panic in his voice. "They took my sister, and threatened to kill her if I didn't do as they ask."

Thog'run paused, considering. "Technomancer," he queried, flicking his eyes towards Gloric. "Do you have record of this?"

"Celine Alyawarre," Gloric confirmed immediately, reading from his secondary lens display. "Reported missing from the twins' Kenmore home, on the outskirts of Brisbane, a month ago."

The king held the giant in the air for a moment longer, then dropped him to the now dirty carpet in disgust. Fazgha let her spell expend itself, tucking the mortar and pestle back in her pocket. She spat on the floor before returning to her place next to the throne.

"Why did they send you?" I asked, daring to speak now that Thog'run seemed to have completed, or at least, paused, his interrogation.

"I have a power," the giant said, panting, from his prone position on the floor. He ponderously put a paw on his bent knee, pushing himself up to a half-crouch. "If you will allow me to display-"

The room exploded with a cacophony of clicks, whirrs, and booms as each of its inhabitants leveled a weapon or spell in the giant's direction, not taking any chances. My ceridium pistol was in my hands and pointed at his heart before the giant could blink.

Thog'run and Damara alone were relaxed, the former staring at the giant with unreadable black eyes and the latter raising a hand that was gently encircled with waves of blue power. In response, a transparent sheen of cobalt vapor appeared around the giant's head, pulsing in time with whatever spell the Inquisitor had prepared.

"I have him," she said, her voice deep and sultry. "Any violence he attempts to commit will first pit his will against mine."

In my years as a Nightpath, I had only seen the spell cast a handful of times. It was a delicate one, allowing the mancer to control the behavior of another being for a brief period, and requiring an enormous amount of willpower and skill to pull off correctly. The Inquisitor was either confident in her ability or reckless in her use of power.

The king nodded, voicing his silent approval, and the giant stood to his full height, towering over the rest of us. Wiping a swarthy hand against his forehead, which was encrusted in sweat, but no longer in blood, he began to sing.

It was a mellifluous chant at first, deep and rich in the giant's baritone that echoed softly in the stone chamber. A simple, wordless melody warmed the air, pleasing in its simplicity.

Slowly, the man began to weave a handful of harmonious notes throughout his spellsong, his voice taking on a number of additive timbres that were haunting, but still beautiful. His eyes began to take on the intense, slightly unhinged glaze that I recalled all too well from the baseball game, and he reached his two big paws towards Damara, indicating that he would need ceridium to complete the mancy.

She complied, reaching within the folds of her robes to hand him two tiny blue gemstones, which disappeared into his huge palms. He nodded his gratitude, continuing the melody as he clapped his hands together, crushing the gems and infusing his chant with magic.

Almost instantaneously, azure dust from the crystals began to encircle his clasped hands, spiraling up his forearms and *into* his nostrils, presumably filling the giant's big lungs. The ceridium, now a fine, glittery powder, then expelled through his mouth as it intermingled with the notes of the spellsong, which had reached a crescendo that sounded earthly and otherworldly at the same time.

"That can't be good for his lungs," Vasshka muttered from around her cigar.

The giant's spell took effect with a flash accompanied by a tiny susurrus of sound that joined his song, now a low chorus that vibrated the king's audience chamber with power. It was the same song that he had been chanting in our battle, and the enchantment encircled his body, providing him with a defensive shield of magic that was transparent, but looked impenetrable. When it reached Damara's vapor, still wrapped around his head, it paused, then snuck underneath the Inquisitor's spell, shattering it from within.

Damara staggered as if struck, her concentration broken so suddenly and with such force that the woman had no opportunity to counter the giant's power. She fell to one knee, not far from the giant, who was now completely covered in the spellsong's shielding enchantment.

I was the first to react, holstering my pistol and drawing my nightblade, intuitively understanding that ceridium bullets would have little effect and unsure whether the sword would do any better.

I closed the distance in an instant, my nightblade ratcheting into full length from its collapsed position in my fist, but the big man raised his hands pacifyingly and dropped the spellsong before I could take action. The shimmering blue outline disappeared from his body, leaving the room heavy with silence in the absence of the haunting melody.

"I've got to get some of *that*," Tribe said aloud,

breaking the tension.

"What was that?" I demanded. I had halted the swing of my sword midway through its arc, and wasn't sure how to proceed. I held the nightblade in the same position stupidly.

The giant cleared his throat, a rumble deep inside his broad chest. "Auromancy," he said. "I've had it since I was a lad, and my sister is...likewise blessed."

Alina stepped forward, intrigued. "What does it do, exactly?"

The auromancer gave a modest shrug as he turned towards her, dwarfing her with his height. Buster walked with the Pitcher, seemingly unperturbed by the turn of events.

"Many things," the man said, a touch of ruefulness in his voice, and I noticed for the first time his Australian drawl. "Mostly of a defensive sort. It can absorb ceridium to meld with its power, and strengthen an inanimate weapon in my hands."

I remembered the greatsword that he had wielded with deadly power. "That checks out," I remarked, finally clicking my nightblade back into its retracted position and stashing it at my waist. Thog'run, who had been quietly watching the scene, sat back on his throne and resumed his statue-like position with one hand on his greataxe.

"Explain, Nightpath," he said, still using my title from when I worked for NIGHT, even though I had been Aurichome's Chief of Intelligence for over a year. I think he knew that it irked me.

"Well," I said, thinking fast, "whoever planned the attack chose the time, place, and method very carefully. They wanted you to be exposed, either because they couldn't challenge you here in Aurichome..."

"Or because they wanted the world to see," the king finished for me.

I nodded. "Knowing where to find you would be one thing, but being able to pull off an attack is another. Judging by the size of their force and their ability to secure seating near the royal family, they must be well-connected enough to know what kind of security to expect."

"Ceridium weaponry is standard among NIGHT agents as well as our aurikar elites," Gloric said thoughtfully from his little platform.

I nodded again, letting everyone chew on the thought for a moment. Belatedly, Tribe moved over to Damara, helping the Inquisitor up from where she crouched, still panting in pain. She stood with some difficulty, wiping her nose with a delicate hand. It came away bloody.

"So the big guy's spell," Vasshka drawled, seeming unimpressed, "it absorbs bullets?"

"Ceridium ones, yeah," I said, looking to the giant, who nodded. "They must have picked him up and kidnapped his sister to cut a path to the king, knowing that they could abduct the crown prince in the process."

"Who, though?" Alina queried, her hand resting absently on Buster's bushy grey mane. "Who would have the resources to set all of this up?"

"Or the motive," I added, my eyes narrowing. Only two potential culprits came to mind, and whereas one had been court martialed *in absentia* and couldn't be tracked anywhere on the network, the other had been imprisoned in the bowels of Aurichome for over a year. Neither made sense.

"Maybe the Unaligned?" Tribe said tentatively, attempting to slide his hand through the crook of Damara's arm to help steady her. She shooed him away irritably.

"Who?" the queen, who had been quiet with her thoughts, said from next to the throne. Her eyes were dark, brooding.

Tribe shook his head, his piercings jangling. "I don't know much about them," he began. "The circles I run in have been talking a lot about them, though. They're dissatisfied with the ongoing wars between aurics and humans, and are trying to screw things up, from what I hear."

I stifled a snort. When I had met the king's adoptive nephew, it had been at an illegal Oxidium dispensary in a seedy area downtown that was known for black markets, mercenary outfits, information dealing, and worse. Old habits stood the test of time, it seemed.

"That has a high probability of being correct," Gloric agreed, tapping away at his keyboard. "Your Highness, if I may project?"

The king nodded from his throne.

Gloric pressed a key, and an augmented reality projection appeared in front of him, bathing the space with a three dimensional image of a crudely scribbled, handwritten flier stapled to a molding wooden post.

"Our informants have found a handful of these fliers posted in the undercity and above," the gnome said, referring to the cavernous warrens where the majority of San Francisco's auric population still lived. "They don't have any identifying markings, but one informant at least indicated that they had heard of a splinter group using that name."

I moved closer to him, examining the image from all sides. It was a minimal, hastily scribbled note that had a couple of short phrases surrounded by an incomprehensible combination of words and numbers. I couldn't make heads or tails of what the coded language meant, but the intelligible phrases were unmistakable in their message, and sent a chill down my spine.

"Read it aloud, Nightpath," the king commanded from his throne.

I squinted, reading the scribble line by line.

"It says *bool isRevolution...equals sign...false...uhm...*"

Gloric made an exasperated noise and clicked a button on his keypad, causing the digitab in my jacket pocket to beep, along with several others in the room. I pulled mine out and walked over to the throne, the AR holodisplay rendering the sign in the air in front of me:

```
bool isRevolution = false;

string answer;

if (!isRevolution) {

    cout << "Unaligned?";

    cin >> answer;

        if (answer == "Karthax for mayor") {
```

isRevolution = true;

```
    };
```

```
  }
```

The king looked at the holodisplay with his inscrutable black eyes, and I saw my companions around the room pulling out their digitabs to read the render that Gloric had sent them.

"Some kind of code, technomancer?" the king rumbled, examining the note.

Gloric nodded, looking at something on his secondary lens display. "It looks to be a snippet from a larger program, written in C plus plus."

I blinked. I had received a modest amount of hacking training in my time with NIGHT, but had only heard references to C++ a handful of times. It was an antiquated, general purpose programming language that had been used at the turn of the century, before JavaScript, then GoScript, and now, Struct, became the *lingua franca* of both network hacking and server-side systems programming.

"Significance?" Thog'run queried tersely.

The Chief of Technology peered over his secondary lens display. "I'm not sure," he said, uncharacteristically. Gloric usually had an answer for everything.

"You can't read it?" Tribe asked incredulously.

"Of course I can *read* it," Gloric snapped testily. "I just don't understand its significance."

"You can read C plus plus?" I asked, trying to appear as though I knew what I was talking about. "What's the gist, at least?"

Gloric looked at the code again. "In its essence, it's a snippet from a basic input program," he said. "There's a boolean – a binary variable, called *isRevolution*, which, at the beginning of the code, is set to be false."

"Which revolution?" Alina asked, looking at her own digitab. "The one that built Aurichome?"

Gloric shook his head. "I'm not sure. But then there's an 'if' statement, where the program will display a question on some sort of console, and then take an action, based on the answer."

"Unaligned?" I asked.

"That's right," Gloric said. "The program asks the question of whether the person is 'Unaligned,' and waits to receive a response."

"Which is?" the king asked.

"It could be any type of string – a sentence, or a phrase," Gloric explained. "It seems as though the correct answer is the phrase, *Karthax for mayor*, which, upon being inputted..." the gnome trailed off, uncomfortable.

"What will happen?" the queen said, following along with great interest.

Gloric shook his head, the Canterbury cross at his neck gleaming in the chandelier light. "If the correct input is given, the program switches *isRevolution* from false to true."

"What does that do?" Alina asked for the room. We were all doing our best to keep up.

"Essentially," the gnome said, "the program

is providing the user with a passcode question of some sort, and if the user enters the correct phrase as input, the program indicates to its master that the revolution should begin."

"Woah," Tribe breathed.

"Where does the person enter the phrase?" Fazgha asked. "And who is the program's 'master?'"

"It's unclear," Gloric said, glancing over at the queen. "I'll have my techs look at it, but this may be something for the Sigil."

I shifted my weight from one foot to the other, thinking. If there was a new fringe group that was dissatisfied with Aurichome and NIGHT, why would they be passing around notes comprised of antiquated code? And, equally important, why would their passcode be supporting the erstwhile Inquisitor General for mayor, presumably of a city from which he had been forced out?

"How do we get to these Unaligned, Tribe?" Vasshka asked, a pudgy hand resting lightly on the butt of one of her ceridium pistols.

"I don't know, actually," the vanguard replied. "I've heard about them in Columbus-Farrow," he said, referring to the carnivalesque, neon North Beach district of San Francisco. "I can ask around to see what the undercity knows."

The king nodded from his throne, and spoke with command. "Do so. Take a handful of elites with you if you need muscle."

Tribe nodded, shifting the daggers on his belt importantly.

"Technomancer," Thog'run said, addressing Gloric, "contact the Sigil. See what he knows about these Unaligned, and their code.

"Nightpath," he continued, turning slightly in his chair to face me. "Take Hadzic and Lestrage to the Presidio. Bring the auromancer with you, but keep a close watch on him."

I felt my eyebrows rise sharply. "Take him with us, king?" I looked at the giant, who stood solemnly in the middle of the dais, resigned to whatever fate awaited him. "You're not concerned he might-"

Thog'run waived away my concerns. "He may be of use. I'm certain you'll handle him better this time."

I swallowed, knowing a threat when I heard one.

"Your Highness," Damara said smoothly, having recovered her composure. She had been so quiet that I had almost forgotten she was in the room with us. "I'd like to request your permission to join the strike force. It would be my pleasure to assist Aurichome as a show of solidarity after what both our organizations have endured today."

The king waved his hand again, acquiescing. "Fine," he said.

I exchanged a look with Alina, who said nothing, then Vasshka, whose eyes narrowed. She clearly didn't like the idea of the invincible giant and the mind-controlling Inquisitor joining us on a foray into San Francisco's most dangerous, monster-infested district.

I shook my head ruefully, already planning an escape route in my mind.

"Nightpath," Thog'run repeated as we gathered our things to leave the audience chamber. There was a hint of emotion in his voice that I had rarely heard from the ordinarily taciturn king.

I turned to face him, placid on his throne with the queen boring holes into my face from his side.

"Yes, king?"

He cleared his throat, a shadow passing across his tusked face before disappearing into the black pits of his crow-footed eyes.

"Bring me back my son."

FOUR

They cannot destroy me. How can one destroy an idea? I am but a thought on the wind, a shadow in a cloud, a doubt within a whisper. I am the nightmare they dare not speak to their children, lest their fears become manifest.

-Agrid the Destroyer

It was a moody ride out of Aurichome and into San Francisco. After being dismissed by the king, Alina and I exchanged contact information with Damara, who exhibited an extreme amount of interest in the half-auric's pitching ability, and agreed to meet us at the Arguello Gate of the southern Presidio. It was somehow decided that Vasshka would ride in Alina's SUV along with Buster, and the auromancer – Andrew, I had to remind myself – would ride with me, on my two-person cruiser.

Aurichome was just putting itself to sleep as we left the palace, the ceridium engine of my cruiser purring softly as we made our way past the citadel's guardposts and around the traffic circle that connected the main arteries that traversed the underground city. At the heart of the roundabout stood the brutal, twenty-foot stone statue of Thog'run II, his booted foot placed on the throat of a coiled dragon and battleaxe held menacingly in the air to finish the job. I paid it little attention as we drove around the statue and headed south towards San Francisco, but could feel Andrew eyeing it from his seat behind me.

"It really is amazing," he said, his voice full of wonder.

I felt my eyes roll. "What?" I asked gruffly, turning my head to the side slightly so that he could hear me.

"Aurichome," he said, his accent making the word sound like "Orricoome." I reminded myself that, as a human, the auromancer had most likely not spent much time in the underrace slums beneath whatever city he came from, let alone the seat of auric power in the United States.

"Yeah, it's a big deal," I offered.

We settled in for the ride, Andrew taking up most of the space on the back of the cruiser with his huge frame, forcing me to lean uncomfortably over the front panel, which housed all of the electronics and smelled, I noticed for the first time, like plastic. Our route took us through the residential southern end of the city, single-story affordable housing built into sloping stone walls that had been tunneled through the earth a decade prior.

My mind turned to dark thoughts as we drove through the well-paved streets, engaging the cruiser's AG boosters once in a while when we encountered ground congestion to coast along with Aurichome's second level of traffic. A year ago, the previous NIGHT Inquisitor

General, William D. Karthax, had been exposed in a triple-crossing plot to sacrifice San Francisco to Thog'run, only to poison the city's waters with an auric-threatening drug that would devastate the underrace population.

As a Nightpath, I was haplessly thrown into the center of Karthax's plot, and somehow managed to avoid being killed while also helping to expose the erstwhile Inquisitor General's treachery to Thog'run and the wider public. Karthax escaped on a cerucopter to who knows where, and the auric king annexed San Francisco as part of Aurichome, a monumental victory in the expansion of the growing nation.

The drug, known as Oxidium, had once been touted as a cure-all for the phenotypic variation that appeared among the first generation of underraces as a result of ceridium exposure. If you were growing pointed ears, tusks, or horns, or discovering that your child's stature was tracking towards startlingly tiny or abnormally huge, you could take a pill to mollify the underrace gene's effects and look more human again.

That was the pitch, at least, without enough clinical trials over longer periods of consumption to support Oxidium's claims. The drug proved to also have several side effects, including increased strength, speed, and reflexes, along with a long-term psychological spiral into a state of unrelenting, murderous anger, known colloquially as the "rage plague." Ragers, as they would be called, were known for being bloodthirsty shells of aurics that could only be placated by the application of more Oxidium, which continued the vicious cycle.

I shuddered, recalling a living nightmare that I had experienced escaping the clutches of a group of ragers being held captive in the Pacific South NIGHT headquarters' virtual penitentiary. The VPen, a chip that induced its inhabitant into a kind of virtual reality that forced them to relive a punitive experience over and over again, was long known to have been appropriated for interrogative means by government officials, and NIGHT was no different in its approach. Being a law-abiding citizen and agent, I had never experienced the VPen for myself, and didn't plan to.

I couldn't say the same for Karthax's accomplice, a low auric entromancer by the name of Agrid the Destroyer or the Betrayer, depending on whom you asked. He had played the part of lackey in the Inquisitor General's plan to triple-cross whatever agreement had been made with Thog'run, and sent his crew of assassins after me more than once. Agrid and I had tangled at least three times, and although he currently held the balance in number of victories, I had hit him when it counted, and hard. He was taken as a prisoner of Aurichome while Karthax escaped, and presumably still languished in the king's prison.

I shuddered again, this time at what Thog'run would have done with him, having seen the king's brutal treatment of Andrew. I didn't know if Thog'run had access to VPen chips with which to subject prisoners to what amounted to be psychological torture, but I had a feeling that he didn't need them to get his point across.

"How big is this Presidio, then?" the giant

said from behind me, startling me.

"Pretty big," I said curtly, pulling the cruiser to a stop at the southern gate out of Aurichome. An aurikar elite in a guard house checked the credentials of my cruiser through a console, then waved me forward. I returned the salute before easing the cruiser up the ramp that took us out of the auric city and into the North Bay forest above.

The night was cold, a brisk breeze rushing against us as we sped along a quiet, tree-lined highway towards San Francisco, blue light spilling from the cruiser's ceridium engine to mix with the bright rays of headlights and a crescent moon overhead. The forest soon gave way to small, neon aboveground cities that dotted the landscape, inviting and sleepy as the hour crept towards midnight.

I felt, rather than heard, Andrew's gasp of astonishment as we approached San Francisco from the north. A brilliant, orange-hued Golden Gate Bridge loomed in front of us, backdropped by a kaleidoscopic city that bubbled with radiant blue, green, orange, and pink lights. The night sky was clear and crisp, drones and cerujets vying for space among the bright stars and weak moon.

The bridge had recently been renovated and reopened after lying silent and dormant during the protracted struggle between NIGHT and Aurichome, and it looked amazing. I revved the cruiser's AG boosters to hover above the perennial traffic that always seemed to coalesce around the northern entrance to the city, taking a southwesterly route and skirting the edge of the two square miles of the Presidio that most dared not enter. For hundreds of years, it had stood as a military base, until its conversion to a park in the late twentieth century. With the skyrocketing population growth in the twenty-twenties and the appearance of the underraces, it became a campground for aurics as well as humans, and later an illegal testing area for magical experimentation.

Mancers from far and wide came to practice their art, often finding willing subjects from the poor and destitute among the Presidio's inhabitants upon whom to test. It was whispered that even NIGHT had a secret facility deep within the area's environs. The organization was quick to quash such rumors, but the Presidio quickly became a place that was not safe even for its residents, let alone outsiders.

With the advent of the rage plague, things got worse. There were few locations in the city proper that could handle aurics afflicted with the condition or support their Oxidium addiction. The Presidio became a place to which ragers began to be sent, eking out a perverse sort of existence on the meager natural resources that still existed in the overgrown Presidio. Their intermingling with whatever failed magical experiments still crept throughout the forest and underground had forced SFPD to ring the entire region with a twenty-foot-high electrified fence and outlaw any new development within a half mile of its borders.

I suspected that ragers and others still found their way into the Presidio through tunnels from the undercity, but their method of ingress had eluded NIGHT for at least a decade. Some secrets were well guarded, it appeared.

We reached the southwest tip of the Presidio, peeling east off the highway to alight on a frontage road that ran the length of the southern border of the area. To our right were the stolid, brightly lit apartment towers of the Richmond District, and to the left, the gloomy, tree-tangled fences of the Presidio.

"Looks worse than it sounds," Andrew said.

"Mmm," I nodded.

A mile's drive took us to the Arguello Gate, a heavily fortified passage through the fence that still had the red sandstone coloration of its original construction. One ruddy standard hung placidly on the gate's leftmost pillar, almost comical in its prideful inscription, which read:

Presidio of San Francisco
Established 1776

The rest of our party was waiting for us in the little cul-de-sac that abutted the gate, Alina's SUV gleaming black in the light from the Richmond. Damara had pulled her NIGHT cruiser alongside Alina, and was using the delay to talk baseball with the Pitcher through the SUV's driver-side window.

I eased my cruiser to a stop next to the group. "What are you waiting for?" I asked.

"*You,*" Alina said as though the answer were obvious, peering around Damara. I could see Buster crowding the cab of the SUV, all but sitting on Vasshka, who looked uncomfortable in the passenger's seat.

I clicked a button on my cruiser's center console, which was linked to my digitab. The console dispatched my credentials to the guardhouse adjacent to the gate. The handful of guards, who didn't ordinarily see a lot of action, looked out of the structure curiously as I led our little caravan up to the gate, which raised as we approached.

I lifted a hand perfunctorily as we drove through, receiving a halfhearted wave in return.

"King's people," I heard one of the guards say, then drove into the Presidio, the gate closing behind us silently after admitting Alina's SUV and Damara's cruiser.

I hadn't been inside the Presidio proper for a couple of years, and it didn't look like anything had changed. Old, gnarled trees towered over the roadway, heightening the area's claustrophobic sensation of enclosure and blocking out what meager light the night sky could offer. Branches and leaves littered the asphalt, which was itself pocked and cracked from years of disrepair. Our bright headlights shone on abandoned buildings, vehicles, and not a few pairs of eyes that reflected darkly back at us in the night.

There would be people, and other creatures, living not far from the fence, and I wasn't thrilled by announcing our arrival with our bright lights and whirring engines, which, although quiet by mechanical standards, were deafening to my ears in the silence. We veered left onto a service road that circuited what was once a golf course and now no more than a muddy swamp, its fetid aroma hitting me in the face like a brick in the cool night air. I checked our location on the cruiser's console, confirming that we were nearing the coordinates that Gloric had provided.

"Eskander to HQ," I said, enabling the communication device in my ear. "We're on the north side of the swamp, approaching the extraction point."

"I see you, Nightpath," Gloric's voice piped in my ear, the gnome following our location on his digitab from Aurichome. It irritated me that everyone, except Alina, seemed to prefer to call me by my previous title, because Thog'run did so. I gritted my teeth.

"Any news from the Sigil?" I asked, trying to be quiet but still curious.

There was a pause, which I took to mean concern on the technomancer's part. "Not really," he said. "The Scribe," Gloric continued, speaking about the Sigil's personal note taker and attendant, "just said that he would look into the code and let us know if he found anything."

I frowned. The Sigil was an early model autonomous vacuum-shaped artificial intelligence whose network extended far beyond those of Aurichome and NIGHT combined. Gloric was often in contact with him, or with his human Scribe, when the technomancer wasn't able to obtain intel on behalf of the king, and if the Sigil didn't know anything about the Unaligned and their cryptic message, I couldn't think of where we'd turn for more information.

My mind continued to follow dark paths as we came to a spot a quarter of a mile north of the swamp, a dead end in the road that was covered by brush and a fallen oak tree the size of a small tower. Gloric's coordinates locked on a small two-story building that was a hundred yards off the road down a driveway past the roadblock, barely visible in the gloom.

I eased my cruiser in a tight semicircle in front of the roadblock, the vehicle lumbering under Andrew's added weight, and cut the engine, signaling for Alina and Damara to do the same. We gathered on the sidewalk at one end of the fallen tree, Buster trotting up happily in front of the rest of the party while Vasshka brought up the rear, a lit cigar in her hand.

"A sniper could see that from a mile away," Damara was haughtily chiding the dwarf as the group approached.

"I'll take my chances," Doubleshot snickered, unconcerned.

I led the way around the fallen oak, stepping onto the overgrown path that led away from the road and towards the building. I winced as branches crunched underfoot, unholstering my pistol and signaling for the others to do the same. Out of the corner of my eye, I saw Andrew unsheathe the greatsword from his back, which made me uncomfortable.

The building stood lightless and lifeless, the width of a soccer pitch in front of us, and I wasn't about to go in there guns blazing without a plan. I raised a fist to halt our movement.

"I'll recon," I said quietly as I turned back to the group. "Vasshka, take Andrew to the far side of the entrance to make sure we're not being flanked. Alina, you and Buster approach from this side with Damara-"

"Shouldn't we have figured this out beforehand?" Andrew interrupted.

I gave him a look. "Would you rather be in jail, big man?"

He shrugged, conceding the point.

We filtered into the night, Vasshka's dual ceridium pistols leading her way with Andrew to the left of the building while the others moved to the right. I drew a ceridium capsule out from my jacket and crushed it, concentrating while murmuring words of power that I had learned from my time in NIGHT.

A cooling sensation came over my body as the magic took effect, cloaking me in shadows and obscuring me from all but the most discerning eye. I crept forward, my pistol pointed towards the sky as I scanned the area. Alina led Damara and Buster around the right side of the driveway, the Pitcher holding her ceridium returning orb in her right hand. Vasshka and Andrew were no more than silhouettes to my left, the dwarf's cigar a pinprick that bobbed as she half-walked, half-crouched towards the side of the building.

The structure itself was unimaginative, a service building of some sort for the onetime golf course. Thick black cracks intermingled with vines that were apparent upon its mildewed walls even at this distance in the dead of night. An owl hooted from somewhere deeper in the Presidio, incongruous with the eerie silence.

"This is a trap," Vasshka's voice buzzed in my earpiece.

"I agree," Alina said.

"Does anyone have anything *useful* to report?" I murmured quietly, receiving no response.

I glided further down the driveway, a shadow against the night, my footsteps silent on the broken asphalt underneath. My enhanced lens display could barely pick out the forms of my companions flanking the building, awaiting my approach.

The building, old and decrepit from disuse, had a small landing with concrete steps leading up to a troll-sized wooden door, which had been left slightly ajar. The stairs were pocked with age and scarred from what looked like the movement of some type of machinery, and several of the door's inlaid square windows had been broken. A soft blue light, barely discernible even at this distance, emanated from within.

"The giant says his sister's definitely in there," Vasshka said in my ear. "He says he can *feel* it," she added dubiously.

"What the hell does that mean?" I whispered.

"I can feel something too," Alina said. As a half-auric, she was more sensitive to ceridium than I was.

"On my command," I said, creeping gingerly up the steps and onto the landing.

The smell of must and mold wafted out of the open door as I drew nearer, the broken glass windows gaping like tiny monstrous maws. I gently pushed the door open with the tip of my pistol, squinting slightly to make out the shapes beyond in the gloom.

I felt myself take in a small breath, confusion warring with emotion at the sight in front of me. The inside of the building, no more than a large room with a crumbling set of stairs at its rear, was in the same state of disrepair as its exterior, stripped to the bones of furnishings. Once colorfully painted walls were peeling and smudged with some dark substance, lit softly by a cold blue light emanating from the center of the room.

A wooden chair had been planted in the middle of the building's dirty linoleum floor, at odds with the room's lack of furniture or ostentation. A young woman slumped on top of it, unmoving but without any clear restraints holding her in place. Dark curls cascaded down her drooping head, covering her face as well as a collar that was attached to her neck. The band was affixed with a glowing ceruchip, the source of the room's only illumination.

"Eskander? What's in there?"

I jumped at the sound of Alina's voice in my ear. The spell of my apprehension broken, I crept forward into the room to take a closer look.

The girl was no more than a teenager, with features and a complexion that were clearly of a kind to Andrew's. Her broad face looked peaceful and she appeared to be sleeping or drugged, without pain, but I didn't like the look of the collar that encircled her thin neck.

"She's here," I breathed. "Anything going on out there?"

"Nothing," Vasshka replied. "We'll come in."

I nodded to myself, crouching in front of the girl and carefully searching around her chair for any obvious traps. Finding none, I gently checked her pulse and confirmed that she was sleeping, with no signs of trauma or injury.

I was examining the collar when the rest of the party entered the room, Vasshka's cigar adding an orange glow to the ceruchip's blue light. Andrew rushed forward, his huge frame quivering with anger.

"Celine," he whispered, pain inflecting his deep voice. "What did they do to her?"

I shrugged, prodding at the collar. "Doesn't look like they've done anything," I said, feeling a prickle as the magic on my body wore off, my cloak of shadows dissipating into dust. "Not sure about this collar, though."

"Some sort of VPen chip?" Alina asked, holstering her ceridium orb. Buster padded up to the girl, sniffing with concern.

I shook my head, having an intimate familiarity with VPen visors from my time in NIGHT. "I don't think so, unless NIGHT has produced a new type of hardware." I turned to look at Damara, a question in my eyes.

The Inquisitor shrugged, her expression dark and noncommittal.

"Can you remove it?" Andrew asked urgently. "Why is she sleeping? Did they drug her?"

"I'm not certain," I responded truthfully to the auromancer's questions. I reached behind the girl's neck, feeling for a clasp of some sort. "Vasshka, will you watch the door?"

The dwarf nodded, taking a spot right inside the doorway, her dual pistols trained on the driveway beyond.

I fiddled with the collar, finding at last a small catch at the base of her neck, which clicked audibly as I unfastened it. The collar fell away into my hands, heavy and metallic.

"That seemed to work," I said.

Almost immediately, the girl's eyes fluttered open, brown and doe-like. They looked blankly around the room until settling on the giant, widening slightly.

"Andrew?" Celine asked haltingly, her voice thick. "What-"

The collar beeped, its magical trigger activating. I looked at the thing stupidly, not understanding.

The girl's body went rigid, some latent spell released by the collar taking hold of her body. Andrew was quick to react, sweeping her into his big arms as she nearly fell from the chair, her head jerking back as she opened her mouth to scream.

"The hell?" Alina exclaimed, giving voice to my thoughts.

To this day, I will never forget the sound that emerged from Celine's slight body at that moment. A shriek, piercing and magical, rent the night, and I dropped the collar out of surprise, covering my ears.

A blue vapor, ceridium from the collar, escaped the ceruchip to mingle with the girl's voice, not unlike Andrew's auromancy but terrifying in its power. Her scream grew in timbre and shook the walls of the building, pouring out of her body in the shape of an azure cone that was painful to watch as it was to hear.

"Cover her mouth!" I shouted, knowing all too well the kind of attention the sound would attract in the quiet Presidio.

To his credit, Andrew attempted to smother the sound with a meaty paw, but was blasted away from Celine's body with the attempt, his hand smoking. The girl slumped to the floor, her back against the chair, the blue cone forming into an oblong portal with shimmering shapes moving within.

The magic took hold in an instant, Celine's innate power coerced by the collar's latent spell into creating a gate into the ether, the realm beyond appearing familiar and strange at the same time. Within, I could see vague shapes suggestive of an age long past mixed with visions of the future and what looked like the dungeons beneath Aurichome. Peering into the portal was like trying to discern movement at the bottom of a lake, but one image stood out clearly amidst the rest: that of a white auric, cloaked in crimson and malevolence, stalking the halls of Aurichome amidst terrible carnage and out into the ether.

As quickly as it had begun, the spell ended, Celine's mouth clattering shut painfully and the room dropping into darkness. The girl collapsed against the floor, her magic spent and head lolling to the side.

"Nightpath!" Gloric was buzzing in my ear, still painfully ringing. "What's happening over there?"

I shook my head, trying to clear it from the pain. "Some kind of spell on the auromancer's sister," I said. "No sign of the prince here."

"There's been a breach in the caverns below," he said, referring to Aurichome's dungeon. "Elites are containing it, but the king wants you to return a-sap."

"We've got company," Vasshka shouted from the doorway.

"Piss," I cursed.

From outside the building, snarls could be heard, feral howls mixed with the buzz of magic.

I looked to Andrew, who was slowly standing, clutching his injured hand to his chest.

"Can you grab her?" I said, motioning to the comatose Celine.

He nodded curtly, gritting his teeth with pain and scooping her up in the crook of his arm like a ragdoll.

"Get to the cruisers!" Alina yelled, following Vasshka through the doorway, the dwarf already firing her pistols as she burst into the night.

I waited for Andrew to lumber out onto the landing before grabbing Damara by the arm. "Don't hold back," I cautioned, knowing the Inquisitor would be more than happy to throw a handful of Aurichome's representatives to the wolves under duress.

She pulled her arm away roughly. "I'm in as much danger as you, Nightpath," she said cryptically, undoubtedly using my previous title to remind me of past loyalties. I really hated that.

I followed her out over the landing and onto the driveway, being greeted by a grisly scene. A dozen or more ragers, their mouths twisted in frothing snarls and their wide eyes gleaming ferociously in the gloom, raced after Vasshka. The dwarf jumped, tumbled, and somersaulted among them like a demon, her pistols flashing every few seconds as they riddled the ragers with silent ceridium bullets.

One of them, a troll, had peeled off in the direction of Alina and Buster, flanked by two weird and wild beasts, boar-looking things that had wicked antlers and that seemed to phase in and out of space, appearing two feet to the right or left of their position of a moment prior. The source of the buzz became apparent every time they shifted, some strange magic causing them to thrum with power.

The Pitcher already had her ceridium orb in her hand, winding up and throwing it with deadly force as it crossed the distance to hit the troll square in the mouth. It left a trail of cobalt smoke in the air as the ceridium chip within activated on impact, returning it to her hand for another volley.

The troll, howling in agony at its broken jaw, dashed forward, its giant claws extended forward. Alina's orb struck again, this time curving unerringly to hit its cheek with a sickening crunch before reappearing in her waiting fist.

I fired my pistol, leaving a smoking hole in its arm while running to the left, attempting to flank it and the boar-like beasts. Buster raced to intercept one of them, tangling with it in a cloud of teeth, claws, and fur, while the other one ran towards me, sensing a new threat.

I shot at it wildly, shifting my pistol to my left hand and drawing my nightblade with my right. The thing was on me in no time, having covered the distance in a flash, and it was terrifying. It was the size of a pony with spiny, porcupine-like hair and rust-colored eyes and teeth, smelling of musk and brimstone. It snapped at me with piranha-like teeth, forcing me to shift my weight awkwardly to avoid losing an arm.

I brought my sword down in front of me in a sweeping motion, more to create space between myself and the monster than to do any real damage. The beast ran right through it, phasing out of the way at just the right moment so that my blade cut air and nothing else. The thing snarled, spitting blue sparks, and took another bite, catching my long coat and tearing a hole in the armor-laced fabric.

I retreated further, trying to position myself in the direction of the cruisers without turning my back to the monster. I feinted backwards and then sprung, thrusting my nightblade forward and being rewarded with a sizzle as it struck the boar-beast in the shoulder. The phasing seemed to have a rhythm, and if I timed my strikes correctly, I could hit the thing while it was in this reality and not whatever hell that spawned it.

The monster jumped suddenly, using its powerful legs to propel it forward. I dropped, avoiding its snapping jaws but getting clipped on the ear by one of its hind claws. It skidded to a stop on the driveway beyond me, blocking my path to the cruisers but far enough away that I felt confident to take a shot with my pistol.

The ceridium bullet hit the beast square in the face, and seemed to get *absorbed* by whatever magic that was enabling its phasing ability. I spat in disgust, quickly holstering my pistol while grabbing the nightblade with both hands.

The monster charged anew, and I pivoted like a bullfighter, waiting for it to phase out and back into reality before bringing my sword down and to the right, shearing its grotesque head clear from its shoulders. Body and head tumbled to the ground, shimmering with magic once again before laying still.

I shook the blade curtly, spattering blood and ichor onto the pavement, before turning to see how the others were faring.

Vasshka had slowed somewhat in her tumbling, but continued to bound out of the way of the ragers, having fallen half of them with her pistols. Alina and Buster had disposed of the troll and other beast, but the Pitcher's non-throwing arm hung limply at her side, bloody with scratches. The pair was attempting to cover the escape of Andrew, who was running towards the cruisers painfully slowly, burdened as he was with his sister's comatose form.

A chorus of whoops and snarls echoed from the far side of the building as a second group of ragers rounded the corner, clamoring with earnest as they sighted battle and blood. My shoulders slumped with the recognition that we would have to fight our way out of there, and were grossly outnumbered.

I ran to take a position alongside Alina, when I saw Damara from the side waving her arms in an arcane gesture, words of power spouting from her lips.

The Inquisitor crushed a ceridium tablet in between her hands, finishing her spell with a clap. A speck of light emerged from her palms, spearing towards the center of the newcomers and striking the ground in their midst. It exploded on impact, creating a thirty-foot sphere of destruction that all but immolated the majority of the ragers, leaving crumbling, smoking husks behind.

"That'll work," Alina said disgustedly from between clenched teeth.

We turned heel and ran for the cruisers,

Vasshka distracting the remaining ragers as we retreated and Buster nipping at their heels like a sheepdog. I quickly overtook Andrew and sheathed my weapons, grabbing at my digitab to start my cruiser's engine and that of Alina's SUV, which was also synced to my tablet. I reached the SUV first, blood streaming from my torn ear and down my jacket, and ripped open the passenger doors, helping Andrew place Celine in the rear seat and ushering the giant into the front as Buster hopped in to join them.

Alina rounded the vehicle and jumped into the driver's seat, gunning the engine and backing away from the roadblock at a dangerous clip. She turned it around with a loud screech and drove away, with Damara trailing her closely on her NIGHT cruiser. I jumped onto my own cruiser, skidding it into position and waiting for Vasshka, who had led the ragers sideways into the forest.

"Get moving!" she shouted as she burst onto the roadway twenty feet in front of me, running backwards while firing into the group of monsters.

I peeled forward, driving as quickly as I dared towards her. She timed her run perfectly, hoisting herself up to the back seat of the cruiser and positioning her back to mine, firing bullets two at a time as I drove us out of range and back onto the main road.

"I love my job," she said as she holstered her weapons and turned around in her seat to face forward. I heard her light a cigar, having seemingly misplaced the previous one in the melee.

"Repeat, *what is your location?*" Gloric was

saying insistently in my ear. "The king wants you back here *now!*"

"On our way," I said, letting out a long breath. Thog'run would not be happy with us returning empty-handed.

FIVE

We do not pick our families – we are born to them, and they to us, even those that we do not produce by our own biology. Our enemies, however, we make by choice.
                    -Fazgha Hezdottr, Queen of Aurichome

"They came in through here," Gloric was saying, tracing a dark finger along the cold stone wall of the Aurichome dungeon. Blood had begun to crust against the flat, otherwise unmarred surface, the only indication that a battle had been fought in that location just hours before.

Dawn was breaking in the world above Aurichome as we gathered, far below the king's audience chamber, in a prison that few aurics or humans entered, and fewer still were able to leave. It was no more than a long corridor, sparsely lit by recessed lamps overhead, and utterly bereft of sound or ornamentation. Steel doors lined one wall of the corridor, each enabled with secured digilocks that pulsed rhythmically with cold blue light, pregnant with enemies of the crown.

The dungeon was more crowded than usual, with a pair of aurikar elite guards flanking the king as he fumed at the turn of events while our little group shifted nervously. One chamber – Agrid's, presumably – stood open and dark, its heavy door soot-laced and lying on the concrete floor of the room, blasted from its hinges.

"Through…the wall," Tribe said incredulously, his normally mischievous face etched with concern.

Gloric nodded, projecting the AR footage from the security feed from his digitab into the air in front of him. It showed a portal of some sorts, not dissimilar to the one that appeared above Celine in the Presidio, forming along the dungeon wall, from which spilled a handful of assassins that I didn't recognize. They looked both auric and human, and made short work of the four aurikar elite guards that were stationed in this corridor at all times. One of them, a dwarf, worked a digitab that almost instantaneously disabled the digilock of Agrid's cell, then stood back as a human pyromancer blew the physical door from its hinges with a fireball. The other assassins clambered into the chamber, returning with a shackled and bedraggled low auric, battered and wastrel thin but unmistakably identifiable by his ghost-white skin.

A troll was waiting for them, casting a terramancy spell as the dwarf used her digitab to unlock Agrid's bindings. The terramancer completed his incantation, healing green light trickling over Agrid's pasty skin and restoring some of the low auric's color. He shook himself, stretching, and then accepted from the pyromancer a long, crimson jacket and spear with which I was all too familiar. He stepped into the portal without a backwards glance, followed by the other assassins before it closed soundlessly.

The whole thing was impeccably coordinated and had taken less than a minute.

"What the hell kind of magic is that?" I asked about the portal that appeared in the middle of a concrete wall.

"I'm a technomancer, not an encyclopedia," Gloric chided.

"It looks like one of Celine's spells," Andrew said, his voice flat and uncomfortable. He had already spent a couple of hours in the dungeon and was evidently not enthused by his quick return.

"Explain," Thog'run said laconically, crossing his burly arms in front of him.

"She has a power like mine...but not like mine," the giant said haltingly, fearful under the king's piercing gaze.

"Auromancy?" Gloric asked, encouraging him to continue.

Andrew shook his head emphatically. "No," he replied. "She's deaf. Can't hear a thing, let alone carry a tune."

I considered the irony that the big man could make magic out of sound, while his sister could hear none of it.

"She's still little, and can't control it yet," he continued, "but sometimes she can do things with time, if she's around ceridium. Make you stand still and forget what you were doing for a tick, or tell you something vague about what's going to happen tomorrow. That sort of thing."

"Time magic?" I asked, considering the frail teenager that we had found slumped in the

Presidio earlier. She had been taken to the king's private hospital, the royal physicians tending to her wounds with Alina's help as a terramancer.

"I'm going to be the first to call it 'chronomancy,'" Tribe piped, looking proud. "Write it down, Gloric."

"Beat me to it," Vasshka said.

Gloric looked thoughtful. "I suppose it's possible," the gnome said. "With a suitable conduit and power source, one could create a temporal displacement that had spatial implications, as well."

"English, please," I implored, having become used to his arcane explanations that no one else understood.

"I'm actually not sure," he said. "But if she has the ability, it's theoretically possible that with enough ceridium, she could create a gate in *time*, that acted as a doorway in *space*, allowing passage through it while the spell is active."

"Space, like outer space?" Tribe asked.

Gloric flipped his hand irritably. "Not *outer* space. Just space."

"Teleportation," I clarified, being familiar with the concept from my limited shadowmancy spells.

The gnome nodded. "Precisely, although over greater distances than normal."

"How'd they do it?" Vasshka asked.

"And who's 'they?'" Tribe added.

"Show them the message, technomancer," Thog'run rumbled.

Complying, Gloric tapped his digitab, projecting the handwritten note that we had seen the previous night with the code scrawled on it. "Remember this?"

I nodded. "Sigil figure out what it is?"

Gloric shook his head uneasily. "The Sigil's still dark. But I was able to find an Unaligned subnetwork that was heavily encrypted, and worked my way past the firewall."

"How'd you do it?" Tribe asked breathlessly.

"How's your server-side Struct knowledge?" the gnome retorted, not receiving an answer. "I'll spare you the details."

"Can we get on with it?" I asked, impatient to unravel the mess in which we had found ourselves.

"Right," Gloric continued. "The Unaligned have a private network that operates on Struct, but has hooks for its users to patch in the C plus plus code that we found. It's a pretty simple API, and all you have to do is replace the 'answer' string with-"

"I thought we were skipping the details," Vasshka complained.

Gloric looked exasperated. "When you patch in the code, you receive this message."

He tapped a button, and a face that I hadn't seen in over a year appeared, hovering above the digitab. William D. Karthax, the former NIGHT Inquisitor General who had been convicted of treason *in absentia*, stared out at an unseen audience, spouting a pre-recorded message in his militaristic, clipped voice.

"My fellow Americans," the recording said, "Our country is rent by the sectarianism promoted by Aurichome and NIGHT. I, myself, fell prey to this bi-partisan fundamentalism, and it has taken me a decade to extricate myself from the bureaucracy and into the light."

He had put on a few pounds, letting his ordinarily close-cropped silver hair grow long, and it flopped over the top of his head untidily. The AR projection made his face look ruddy, almost orange, as he spoke with the fervor of a beseeching politician.

"If you feel, like I do," the recording continued, "that the great city of San Francisco, once a bastion of human progress and technology, is now a bureaucratic swamp that has been polluted by the touch of bi-partisan politics, then share this message with the people you love. Vote for me as mayor this coming election, and together we'll drain the swamp of the influence of Aurichome and NIGHT, and restore San Francisco to her former glory."

The message went on to spout several more aphorisms denouncing the current political situation and aggrandizing Karthax's achievements as a war hero and the counterpoint offered by the so-called Unaligned, before signing off and repeating the speech anew.

Gloric clicked his digitab, cutting off the recording in disgust. The dungeon, already solemn to begin with, was silent with contemplation.

"This doesn't seem good," Tribe was the first to break the stillness.

"It's not," I agreed. I had reported to Karthax for several years, and he had proven to be a capable and crafty leader of humans in his austere way, flawed as he was in his xenophobia.

"Doesn't matter if no one listens to him," Vasshka offered.

"It unfortunately seems as though some do," Gloric countered. "Both my technicians and Tribe's contacts confirm that the Unaligned have quite the following, both outside and within the city."

"Karthax's reach still extends far beyond his person, it seems," Thog'run rumbled ruefully. I could sense that the erstwhile Inquisitor General's triple-cross still rankled with the auric king.

"His, and the Betrayer's," Alina's voice rang from the entrance to the dungeon. I looked up to see the guards stationed at the giant steel portal move to the side deferentially, the Pitcher stepping between them with Buster, and a very demure Celine, in tow.

Andrew's eyes lit up at the sight, and he rushed to his sister, crouching slightly to embrace her. Buster, excited by the reunion, pranced nearby, sniffing at the couple.

"Damara checked in with NIGHT before she returned to their HQ," Alina explained as she joined us. "The assassins loyal to Agrid have fallen in with the Unaligned, having already sided with Karthax during Project Watershed."

The report made sense, given that Agrid and Karthax had worked together to betray both Aurichome and NIGHT to their own benefit a year ago. That they had found support – or had been fomenting it – in a third, non-partisan faction was no surprise.

I felt as though a vague, threadbare outline of their machinations was slowly taking form, but couldn't make sense of it with so many questions unanswered. I decided to voice a few of them.

"One thing I've never understood," I said, "is Agrid's motivation. What does he gain from siding with Karthax?"

I thought it was a fair question. Karthax's aim had become clear during Project Watershed: rid the city of aurics as efficiently as possible, restoring it to a human community where he himself held absolute power. Why a low auric entromancer would take up as his lackey, or, at best, his equal, was beyond me.

"Chaos," Thog'run said simply, surprising me by being the first to respond. I turned to him.

"King?"

Thog'run shrugged, letting his arms fall from his chest and looking – if such a thing could be said about the stoic auric king – tired. He paced away from the guards that flanked him, peering enigmatically into the empty jail cell.

"He is the queen's brother," he said simply, as though the admission explained everything. Alina and I shared a wide-eyed look that said, *if you knew about this and didn't tell me, we're* done.

"We fought together, in the Third Gulf War," he continued, reliving something to which none of us, save perhaps Alina, could relate. "It was before Fazgha and I were married." He waved a meaty hand to indicate the area around him, presumably all of Aurichome. "Before all of this.

"We shared a vision of an auric nation, where the underraces could extricate themselves from their second-class citizenry and create a future for themselves out from under the boot of their human counterparts."

He smirked, an unnatural expression on his dour, tusked face. "It was a dream that we shared, but whereas I believed humans should be allowed to participate in the building of Aurichome if they swore fealty, the Destroyer took an exclusionary path."

I had never heard more than a few curt words at a time from the laconic king, and it made me nervous. None of us dared interrupt as he continued his story.

"He was studying an occult form of magic based on chaos – what you refer to as 'entromancy' – and threatened, in the heat of a disagreement we once had on the treatment of a NIGHT agent that we captured, to use it on the human. You have seen how I deal with threats."

He looked pointedly at Andrew, who gulped almost comically, still crouched with his sister. I noticed that the giant was silently signing for Celine, relating Thog'run's words to her.

"I threw him out for his insubordination, and he viewed it as a betrayal. If I know his heart, he'd rather sow violence and confusion rather than see Aurichome reach its true, multiracial glory, even if doing so means siding with Karthax, who represents the antithesis of our shared dream."

Agrid's words rang out to me from one of our encounters a year ago. *Do not speak to me of traitors*, he had yelled, sheathed in rage and power. I shivered, understanding.

"I think the entromancy has corrupted him," Thog'run added, his voice grating like boulders on more stone. "One who cavorts with chaos cannot help but be tainted by it."

It was a lot to take in, but I started to do

what the king had hired me to: take disparate strands and weave them into a tapestry that made sense.

"So, Agrid holds a long-standing grudge and is willing to continue to work with Karthax to throw Aurichome and NIGHT into disarray," I said. The king looked up as I spoke. "And Karthax, having failed at triple-crossing Aurichome and being ousted by NIGHT, is attempting to rally whoever's left to take control of the city."

"Humans," Vasshka said, scrunching her nose.

"Maybe," I hedged, not knowing what the Unaligned constituency looked like. It was too early to tell, and people had a history of following whosoever spoke the loudest.

"What I don't understand," I continued, enumerating a short list on my fingers, "is how they were able to get a time magic portal-"

"Chronomancy," Tribe corrected me.

"OK, how they were able to get a *chronomancy* portal," I yielded, "to appear in the first place, let alone in one of the most protected areas of Aurichome."

"It has to be the collar," Andrew's deep, mellifluous voice filled the corridor. He stood, his head nearly touching the low ceiling. "They put the collar on her and forced the magic out of her somehow."

I looked to Alina, who had escorted Celine to the hospital. "The mancers are still testing it," she said unconvincingly. "Could be possible, though, especially if she already knew the spell to be cast."

"I didn't know it," Celine said, in her halting

way, which I now recognized was the voice of someone who had never been able to hear, rather than being a result of her imprisonment. She had been following along with our conversation by a combination of reading Andrew's hand signs and our lips.

"I can only do spells sometimes, but not always, and not always correctly," she explained. "It's frustrating."

"What did they do to you?" Andrew asked gently, signing as he spoke.

"Nothing," she said, taking confidence from her big brother's presence. "At least, I don't remember anything. They put a collar on me and gave me a drug that put me to sleep. When I woke up, you were there," she pointed at me.

"Who's 'they', Celine?" Alina said softly. The young girl seemed to trust her.

"I don't know," Celine said honestly. "I remember a dwarf, who attached the collar to me, and a human, who did some sort of magic on it. The rest are shadows."

I chewed on my lip, remembering the assassins from the security feed. Something else nagged at the corners of my consciousness.

"Gloric," I said. "Can you play the AR recording back?"

"The Karthax one or the security feed?"

"The security cam," I said, not wanting to see Karthax's face again, now or ever.

"You've got it," the gnome piped, clicking a button. The recording played again, holograms entering through the chronomancy portal and escaping with Agrid the Destroyer.

"That's them!" Celine exclaimed, pointing, yet without any signs of fear. She seemed to be a tough sort.

"Again, Gloric?" I ignored the confirmation of the assassins' identities, searching for something. "Just the end part."

The technomancer backed up the recording a handful of frames, just as the assailants escaped through the portal.

"Play that on repeat," I said.

Gloric complied, and the AR hologram cycled, displaying Agrid striding through the portal over and over again, followed by the other assassins, and finally, the dwarf, who touched something on the wall before disappearing into its depths.

"Slow it down?" I asked. "And zoom in on the dwarf."

The hologram magnified, showing the squat, portly dwarf as she followed the others, waving a hand expertly at a small device that was attached to the wall next to the time portal. A bit of magic escaped her fingers, touching the device and rendering it inert as she grabbed it and strolled through the portal before it closed behind her.

"Another technomancer?" Tribe asked.

"Great," Vasshka grunted distastefully.

"That device looks an awful lot like the collar they put on Celine," Alina said.

"It does," I agreed. "But how did they get it in here? And why'd they take us all the way to the Presidio when they could have activated the device from anywhere?"

"Bait and switch," Vasshka shrugged. "Easier for them to throw us off their trail and leave the house unprotected."

"Maybe," I said, unconvinced. "Gloric, can you run the vid back even further? When they brought Andrew in?"

"Sure." The gnome searched his digitab for the appropriate time signature, restoring the camera recording to several hours earlier, when a handful of aurikar guards dragged a battered Andrew through the hallway, followed by Damara, whom I remembered had accompanied them before joining us in the king's auditorium.

It was so imperceptible that I had to ask Gloric to re-display the clip several times, but Damara's movements were unmistakable. Following the guards as they opened an empty cell not far from Agrid's, the Inquisitor moved a step too close to an aurikar elite, dexterously skipping backwards as he turned to put Andrew in the cell. She used the movement to conceal her placement of the device on the corridor wall, feigning as though using the wall for balance.

"Saw that one coming," Vasshka said, recognizing Damara's deception.

"Thanks for not mentioning it to the rest of us," Tribe replied, squinting at the hologram.

"So NIGHT's in on this?" Alina asked, warily eying Thog'run, who was unreadable.

"I wouldn't be so sure," I said cautiously, as much to mollify the king, whose nation had a tremulous relationship with the opposing faction at best, as to speak my own truth. I knew Madge, the current Inquisitor General, and her people well, and couldn't fathom what they would gain by their involvement in such a plot.

"What I'd like to know," Alina continued, "is how in the hell they got past Gloric's defenses and how we haven't gotten wind of *any* of this."

For once, we didn't have long to wait for an

answer. Gloric's digitab beeped on its own, followed by mine, and the rest of the tablets carried by the corridor's occupants.

"Um," I said, picking my digitab out from my coat pocket.

Unbidden, the bust of a thin, ash-white low auric materialized in full hologram above my digitab, overriding the device's security protocols and staring at me full in the face. The image was eerie as it was menacing, as the auric was unassuming, with short black hair and unobtrusively elongated ears and tusks, but there was an air about him that was unsettling.

It was Agrid the Destroyer, and he was speaking to each of us from our personal digitabs.

"Cut the feed," I said imperatively to Gloric.

The gnome looked frantic, tapping away at his little keyboard as the entromancer leered back at him. "I can't," he complained.

"Greetings, Aurichome," the Destroyer said cheerily, his voice sounding like the susurrus of a snake moving through dry grass. "I apologize for waking you from your slumber, but I must deliver a message to your king."

"He's transmitting to everyone in the kingdom," Gloric said, typing furiously, his eyes wide.

"*Stop* him, technomancer," Thog'run commanded, striding with purpose towards Gloric.

"I *can't*," the gnome repeated, his frustration and panic making me twinge.

"King Thog'run," Agrid continued pleasantly, "you have twenty-four hours from this moment to abdicate the throne to me, and accede to my full authority over Aurichome."

Thog'run grabbed Gloric's digitab angrily, throwing it against the stone wall with a roar. It crunched and clattered as the gnome cowered from the king's rage.

"Resist," the entromancer continued speaking from the rest of our digitabs, and throughout Aurichome, "and the crown prince dies."

With that, the hologram disappeared as quickly as it had materialized, and my digitab went blank. The corridor went still, the silence disturbed only by a slight buzzing from the harsh lights overhead.

"Glory," Alina said gently, the first to recover from the shock of what had transpired. "Did you get a read on his location?"

The gnome looked up at her with terror-ringed eyes, still trembling in the shadow of Thog'run, who stared down at the broken digitab in anger, or perhaps futility.

Gloric nodded.

"Where?"

He said two words, sending a chill through my body that nestled in the pit of my stomach.

"Reno," he squeaked, almost a whimper. "Sigil."

The king looked up at that, the gravity of the situation dawning on him as it did the rest of us. He fixed me with a piercing, wrathful gaze, communicating his intent without saying a word.

I stifled a sigh, craving sleep and knowing that it wasn't in the cards for the foreseeable future.

"I'm going," I said.

SIX

01101000 01100101 01101100 01110000.
                              -The Sigil of Sparks

"No, mom," I said, trying to mollify her concern. "I don't plan on being back by dinner time. Just stay safe and don't leave the apartment."

Most aurics and humans were having breakfast by the time I had gotten on the road to Reno, and my family, with whom I hadn't been in contact since the baseball game fiasco, were understandably worried. My brief rehashing of the night's events did little to calm them, even accustomed as they were to my profession's unsavory elements.

"Be *careful*," my father shouted through my mother's digitab. Evidently, I was on speakerphone.

"I'm a *secret agent*, dad," I said, exasperated, engaging my cruiser's autodrive function as I turned east towards Nevada. "I'm *always* careful."

"Don't yell at your father!" my mother's voice admonished. "Just come back safe."

"I'll do my best," I conceded. "Just don't go anywhere until I come back, OK?"

She harrumphed, and I hung up the line.

A cool wind caressed my face as I whipped down the highway, the morning sun overhead painful to my sleep deprived eyes. A few vehicles ahead, Vasshka cruised on her hog, somehow looking lazy and uncommitted as she weaved between and sometimes above the daytime traffic. Behind me trailed Alina in her SUV with a full house that included Gloric, Buster, Andrew, and Celine. Tribe had pleaded his case to accompany us, but the king's will was iron, unwilling as he was to put his adoptive nephew in harm's way with the crown prince's life already on the line.

We had taken some time to devise a strategy, knowing full well that if Agrid was in Reno, he had likely fought his way past the Sigil's defenses and was availing himself of the AI's extensive network that superseded that of even NIGHT or Aurichome. There was no other way that the Unaligned would have been able to pull off their capture of Thog'run III and hack into every digitab in Aurichome without the help of the Sigil or someone equally powerful.

The circles within circles made my tired mind, dulled from the repeated rush and fallow of adrenaline, threaten to spiral out of control. Whoever was pulling the strings – be it Agrid, Karthax, or someone else in the Unaligned – had painstakingly planned each step of their sordid plan, and we had taken the bait at every turn. They had kidnapped Celine to coerce Andrew into working for them, and harnessed the auromancer's unique power to get their assassins near enough to the crown prince to kidnap him. That, in turn, allowed Andrew to be imprisoned in Aurichome's dungeon, giving

Damara, a NIGHT Inquisitor, access to plant the chronomancy device, an admission that would be unthinkable in any other circumstance.

The Unaligned had then led us to a location in the Presidio, which took several of the king's most trusted operatives away from Aurichome and provided a conduit for Celine's forced spellcasting and Agrid's escape. They had anticipated our every move, and had the technological firepower to round out the corners.

The implications were troubling, if not terrifying. On the one hand, Karthax's xenophobic message was being propagated through the distribution of an arcane code, in the hopes of fomenting a human-centric revolution from within San Francisco. On the other, Agrid sought to seize Aurichome by compulsion, with a sizeable bargaining chip in the form of the king's firstborn.

The role reversal was palpable in its irony: the former Inquisitor General, a human public figure, was working in the shadows to move the Unaligned's agenda forward, while a low auric entromancer, whose name was unknown to most, had just made the crown look weak in a devastating broadcast.

I wearily turned my thoughts to the coming encounter. Our strategy, if it could be called that, was little more than a smash-and-grab approach. I would distract Agrid, drawing upon my brief history with him, while the others would get Gloric close enough to use his technomancy to try to circumvent whatever the Unaligned had done to the Sigil's network. Vasshka was tasked with ensuring the crown prince's safety, while Alina, Buster, and Andrew would provide cover for Gloric.

Celine was a wild card, which I was loath to play, even in such dire circumstances. Andrew had proven valuable in a fight, and had made a case for his sister's usefulness in providing us with some breathing room if her powers allowed for it. Alina assured me that the king's physicians had given Celine a clean bill of health, but I was neither convinced that the young girl could control her chronomancy skill on command, nor did I trust her or her giant brother.

I shrugged to myself. They would help us, or they wouldn't. All that mattered was for them to buy us time so that Gloric could work his magic and the rest of us could extract Thog'run III from the Unaligned's grasp.

They undoubtedly knew that we were coming.

The central California landscape whipped by us, stretches of dry, wheat-colored earth pocked by cities and strip malls that disappeared as quickly as they materialized. Slowly, the topography began to rise as we approached the Sierras, passing through a government checkpoint in Truckee and beginning our crawl up the mountains.

A crisp breeze snaked its way down the tree-lined freeway, bringing with it the pine-laced scent of autumn. Vasshka slowed as we approach a once-functional dwarven outpost near the border, her back straightened in solemn, silent grief. We had ridden through the area a year before, when the Destroyer and his crew had also come through, cutting down the guards in their path. Vasshka's brother, Rodder, had been among them.

The outpost lay forgotten and unmanned, the dwarves having pulled deeper into their underground fortresses and away from the outside world. Her respects paid, Vasshka gunned her cruiser and led us into the outskirts of Reno.

The area past the border had been abandoned for a decade or more, human settlements left to rot after the dwarves and other aurics had made Nevada their home. Rusty, overturned vehicles littered the sides of the roadway, with dark, gaping windows looking out of empty buildings that had once supported hundreds of thousands of humans. Unlike our unauthorized visit a year prior, we could have taken a cerucopter through the auric territory without fear of dwarven reprisal, but had agreed that our land vehicles would pose less of a target in case the Unaligned had commissioned some sort of anti-air artillery in anticipation of our arrival.

It took me a couple of minutes to realize that something was off, and the same amount of time to figure out what my subconscious had picked up. For several years, drones had been disappearing from urban centers without explanation, vanishing from the network despite all attempts to locate them. It wasn't until we visited Reno last year that we saw them, orbiting the Sigil's sanctuary within a two-mile radius like pilgrims circumambulating the epicenter of tech power.

As we drove through the outskirts of Reno, coming up on the once-bustling casino town at top speed, it became evident that whatever spell that had been drawing the drones from far and wide had been broken. There wasn't a drone in sight, nor any sign that they had been disabled or depowered. The town was eerily silent without their constant buzzing, and it didn't bode well for the Sigil's safety.

Reno itself was unchanged from our previous visit. Towering casinos blocked out the blue sky overhead, casting AR digads that promoted restaurants, shows, and merchandise that had long been abandoned. It was early afternoon by the time we drove under the arching sign that once read *Reno – The Biggest Little City in the World* and had been hacked to display, in colorful holographic writing, *Reno – The Best City.* Giant, bubbling fountains filled the air with a distinctly chlorinated odor and the city's only sound aside from the low hum of our cruisers and Alina's SUV.

Vasshka guided us to a particularly large casino hotel, pulling her cruiser into a brick-lined, curving driveway that had once served as a valet. We parked our vehicles in front of two massive, tinted sliding doors, stretching our legs before throwing ourselves into what was undoubtedly imminent danger.

Andrew and Celine were wide-eyed as they exited Alina's SUV, following a bounding Buster to the far side of the driveway to look out at the city, dazzlingly lit even under the midday sun. The giant pointed at something, and Celine followed his gaze in wonder, clapping her hands in delight at whatever it was that she saw.

"Tourists," Alina said with a smile as she joined Vasshka and me, a touch of kindness in her voice. I had the feeling that we were too jaded by war and political turmoil to enjoy quiet moments such as these, and the siblings' reaction to Reno surprised me. That they could find wonder in the direst of circumstances gave me hope.

Gloric walked up to us slowly, glum as he examined something on his lens display.

"What's the matter?" Vasshka asked, lighting a cigar as he approached.

The gnome was still rattled from the king's display of anger, and his concern for the Sigil shone clearly on his dark features. "I'm getting a strange reading from within the Sigil's sanctuary," he said.

"Stranger than an artificial intelligence whose network is somehow more powerful than everyone else's combined?" I asked sarcastically.

Gloric nodded. "It's not tech," he faltered, searching for the right words. "I mean, it *is* tech, but it's also magic, and organic at the same time."

"Great," Vasshka opined.

Alina called over the others, unholstering her ceridium orb from its pouch. "Let's go," she said.

The double doors separated as we approached, blasting us with frigid air conditioning and a cacophony of sounds and smells from the casino within. Old cigarette smoke mixed with carpet cleaner and the metal tang of slot machines to assault our senses. Automated gambling cabinets whirred and jingled cheerfully, projecting AR images of gold coins, chiseled bodies, and hot cars, while green felt card tables stood empty and forgotten.

We made our way through the din and down a corridor to a marble archway framed with the word *COLISEVM*, the entrance to an open-air stadium that had been constructed in the shape of a Roman arena. Another set of automatic doors stood between us and the amphitheater, and I stopped us just outside of their range to review the plan.

"Everyone clear on their roles?" I asked, receiving a series of nods.

Andrew alone looked skeptical. "Shouldn't we have a bigger force, or at least some backup?" he asked reasonably.

"Tell it to the king," Gloric said gloomily.

Vasshka nodded. "'Your mess, your cleanup,'" she said, quoting Thog'run's admonition to us before we left.

The auromancer frowned in what I took to mean acquiescence, drawing his greatsword from its sheath on his back.

I turned and walked through the double doors, greeted by the familiar sight of the Sigil's sanctuary.

It was more functional than pretty, with rows of marble benches encircling a large grass pitch that itself was framed by a dirt running track. Tall standing lights were lit brightly even during the daytime, casting fluorescence over the pitch and its mechanical denizens.

There were hundreds of them. Ceridium generators, ancient microwaves, and modern drones were littered amidst all manner of appliances, machines, and even a few vehicles. It was a tech temple of sorts, a reminder of human and auric technology from the earliest carburetor to the most recent iteration of the digitab.

At the arena's center was an oval bed of green, free from the tech litter. The area's usual inhabitants – the Sigil and his bearded human Scribe – were joined by a motley crew, with Agrid at their heart. The entromancer was unmistakable in his crimson jacket and wielding his ebony spear, his presence commanding our attention as we cautiously picked our way in between the detritus and chaff.

We had showdowned in this very casino, with Agrid and his crew besting mine and leaving me and Gloric for dead as they escaped with Tribe. I silently vowed to not let something like that happen again, and to secure Thog'run's firstborn at all costs.

"Hello, Nightpath," the entromancer said in his silky voice as we approached.

"Jackass," I greeted.

He smirked, his lackeys on edge, fingering their weapons as we drew near to the edge of the oval. I stopped right outside, next to an old laundry machine, indicating for my group to do the same.

We were outnumbered, and the situation was more dismal than I had expected. The entromancer was flanked by his assassins, all of whom eyed us with hateful if restrained glares. Agrid had evidently instructed his people to stay their weapons, either for the sake of parlay or because he didn't view us as a threat.

To his right squatted the dwarf technomancer, dressed smartly in black jeans and a leather military-style jacket with unnecessary buckles at the shoulders. Her blond hair was almost white and pulled back behind her slightly pointy ears, revealing small horns just above her temples. She was tapping furiously at a digitab with one hand, holding her other fingers outstretched towards the Scribe to one side of her.

The human had seen better days. The ordinarily thin Scribe looked emaciated, his deep eyes sunken and long beard ratty and tangled. He sat, cross-legged, on his customary circular pillow, his hands cradling a digital tablet and pen, and his entire body bathed in a sharp blue glow that widened and extended from a thin line that emanated from the dwarf's fingertips. The Scribe's mouth moved soundlessly as he stared forwards at nothing, his right hand scribbling blindly at the tablet in his lap.

To Agrid's left was the pyromancer, looking very punkish with a shaved and tattooed head and a stained print t-shirt, his waist encircled by a flannel button-up that had been tied at the front. He held the crown prince like a meat shield out in front of him, the pyromancer's arm around Thog'run III's neck and his palm positioned threateningly next to the auric's face. Power stirred within the pyromancer's hand, indicating that he had readied a spell to blast the prince to bits at a moment's notice.

Thog'run III watched with the same hard stare of his father as we approached. He looked uncomfortable, stooping a little under the arm of the shorter pyromancer, but unharmed, and I reminded myself that Agrid's relation to the queen would make the crown prince his nephew. Perhaps the entromancer himself had limits to the steps he was willing to take to ensure his own success.

An oath escaped Gloric's lips behind me, and I searched the oval to discover what he had seen. A handful of auric and human assassins stood protectively near Agrid, but I knew at once what had drawn the gnome's eye. At the entromancer's feet was the Sigil, a small, round device that had once been an automated vacuum cleaner built at the beginning of the twenty-first century.

It had been smashed into three distinct pieces, cruelly battered and discarded like a forgotten bauble. The LED lights that dotted its surface were utterly dark and lifeless, and wires stuck out erratically through its metal and plastic casing.

"What did you do to him?" Gloric whined, stepping forward. I put out a hand, holding back his small, trembling frame with ease.

Agrid smirked again, his gaze not leaving my face. "Turns out the Sigil was a charlatan, after all," he said cryptically.

"What do you want?" I asked, not wasting any time.

His thin eyebrows rose slightly. "Did you not receive my message?"

I nodded. "Half of the world has seen it by now."

Agrid furrowed his brow. "I made my intentions clear. I want the throne."

"You know that the king will never accede to your demands."

He shrugged. "Then his son dies."

I shook my head. "I don't think that's a risk you'd take, even if you'd be willing to kill your own nephew."

That hit a nerve. A shadow passed over the low auric's eyes, quickly replaced by his customary leer.

I decided to press, taking a step forward, onto the grass oval. The entromancer's lackeys stiffened, and he held a hand up to mollify them, unconcerned.

"I must admit," the Destroyer said, "I didn't realize you were on such...candid speaking terms with my brother-in-law."

It was my turn to shrug. "I work for him now."

"So I hear."

"Why'd you draw us here, then?" I demanded, trying to draw him out while the others readied. I could feel them move between the detritus, taking up positions.

Their movement did not go unnoticed by the assassins, who finally drew their weapons and trained them on my group behind me. A tiny red flame thrummed in the pyromancer's palm, while the dwarf at Agrid's side continued to work whatever magic that was ensorcelling the Scribe.

"If you kill the king's son, you're done," I continued. "You'll have nothing but a bigger target on your back. And if I know Thog'run, he won't give up Aurichome for *anything*."

"You underestimate his familial attachments," the Destroyer countered.

"Perhaps," I conceded. "But that still doesn't explain why you've brought us here. You knew that Thog'run would send an extraction party, and the Unaligned have been leading us around by the nose."

His eyes widened again, this time appraisingly. "I'm impressed," he said, dark humor in his voice. "I would have expected for Aurichome and NIGHT to have taken much longer to discover the identity of my benefactors, and for you to be unknowing for a second time in your role as a pawn."

He tapped his spear against the grass, emitting a dull thud that sent ripples of blue flame up its shaft and sharp blade.

"No matter," he said. "Aurichome will be ours within the day, and the rest of the city shortly thereafter. And yes, Nightpath, I *have* led you here, knowing – or at least, hoping – that my brother-in-law would send you."

"Why?" I asked, genuinely unsure.

He smiled terribly. "To settle our score," he said throatily. "To witness, and to die."

A flash of blue, followed by a chortling sound, stole whatever witty response I had prepared. The pyromancer to Agrid's left gasped, his mouth working soundlessly, a ceridium-ringed hole still burning between his eyes. His spell fizzled into ash in his hand as he fell to the floor, dead.

I looked to my right over the washing machine to see Vasshka, her pistols glowing and leveled at the pyromancer.

"Bored," she said.

Many things happened at once. Having surprised Agrid's minions, my group burst into action, unleashing bullets and magic without hesitation. Vasshka fired unerringly at two other assassins before disappearing into the tech rubble, while I noticed Alina's orb whiz through the air and topple a troll that was lurking on the edge of the oval. Somewhere behind me, Andrew's deep voice rose in song as he took up a spell.

Unfazed by the attack, Agrid called out in the voice of a raven, dropping an egg underfoot to crush it with his boot. A shimmering, quicksilver sheen filled with little hexagons covered his skin, protecting him from attacks. I reminded myself that his form of magic, entromancy, utilized a sort of butterfly effect to bend the powers of chaos to his will, without a manifest power source like ceridium.

One of his assassins, a human, charged at me, and I dropped to one knee, drawing my nightblade in the same motion. The man struggled to slow his movement as my blade escaped its sheath, ratcheting into its full curved form as I drew it diagonally upwards, effortlessly slicing through his torso.

I sidestepped to let him fall as Andrew burst onto the grass, chanting with purpose and making a beeline for Agrid with his greatsword raised for a downward chop. Several ceridium bullets found his body from the assassins' guns and were absorbed harmlessly into the auromancer's glowing outline, the product of his spell. Just finishing his own incantation, Agrid stepped backwards alarmingly, raising a forearm just in time to catch the brunt of Andrew's strike on his quicksilver-shrouded sleeve.

The blow shattered the shield on the entromancer's arm, driving him backwards and sinking his feet several inches into the grass.

Quicksilver from other parts of his body rushed to close the gap that had formed on his forearm, leaving his unnatural armor thinner and more translucent than it had been before.

Andrew swung the greatsword for another chop, but this time, Agrid was prepared. His armor had protected him from the brunt of the initial blow, but his forearm still lay bare through a gash in his crimson jacket, raw with blood. He wiped his other hand across the wound, dropping blood in front of him while barking in some unknown tongue.

His spell took hold as Andrew struck, catching the auromancer full in the chest with the droplets of blood, which elongated into dagger-shaped arrows. The magic, fueled as it was by something other than ceridium, tore through the giant's defenses and rent his torso and chest. He roared with pain, his attack spoiled.

I didn't have time to watch their melee as another assassin, the terramancer troll, began chanting to my left, his eyes fixed on Gloric, who had appeared at the edge of the clearing, a small turret mounted on his shoulder. He was firing at the dwarf technomancer, his face contorted in rage and sorrow, beginning to cast a spell of his own and completely unaware of the troll.

I crushed a ceridium capsule, shadowstepping to the terramancer in an instant and driving my nightblade before me. The troll dashed to the side, wide-eyed, but continued his spell to its completion.

Four spectral beasts, wolves with long, trailing ears and without tails, emerged from the ether and surged towards Gloric, snarling mutely and evilly.

"Gloric!" I yelled, futilely trying to draw his attention.

I felt, rather than heard, Celine's voice lifting into a peal of anger, her voice rising above the clamor of the fight and even Andrew's song. I afforded myself a split second to turn, and saw her standing by the washing machine, a ceridium tablet between her haloed palms, drawing upon its power to fuel her chanting.

The specters slowed in their approach, then stopped altogether a hair's breadth from Gloric's unaware form. Two other assassins in their path stopped as well, frozen in time by Celine's chronomancy.

"That'll work," I heard from my right.

I turned to see Vasshka tumble past me, firing point blank at the terramancer, who was attempting to cast another spell. The troll turned sideways, catching the bullets on his flank and diving into the detritus outside of the oval.

"Thanks," I offered, taking a breath.

She nodded, her wide-brimmed hat bobbling.

"What happened to the plan?" I said.

"You took too long," she complained.

A bang behind me drew our attention, and I turned to see what new hell had been let loose, immediately regretting it.

Agrid's technomancer had completed her incantation, drawing on the Scribe's life force and her own magic to unthinkable effect. She punched a button on her digitab with finality, clenching her fist in triumph.

I grabbed at my coat, attempting to draw

forth another ceridium capsule and shadowstep towards her, but immediately lost my footing as the ground began to shake. I dropped to one knee as the other assassins scattered, evidently expecting whatever devastation the technomancer had planned. Even Agrid stepped away, steadying himself against a standing lamp as a bloodied Andrew fell away from him.

Vasshka alone kept her footing, the spry dwarf riding the bucking and cracking pitch as she attempted to fire at the technomancer, to no avail.

A metallic clatter erupted from well within the earth, the sound of gears grinding against stone. It was as though giant nails were being drawn against a flat chalkboard, painfully loud and otherworldly. I dropped my nightblade, instinctively placing my hands over my ears, and saw Vasshka do the same. The screech reverberated off the arena's stone walls as the ground beneath buckled, vomiting death.

A hand, if it could be called such a thing, thrust through the collapsing earth behind Agrid. It was the size of my cruiser, and had long, skeletal claws that tore the pitch and metal around it into ribbons. It was attached to a foreleg that was composed of rotting flesh and more bone, its tattered muscles straining to pull some monstrosity out of the pit and into our world above.

Terror is a great motivator, and I found my footing, scooping up my nightblade and drawing my pistol. I fired bullet after bullet into the creature as it emerged, to very little effect. With a final heave, it pulled itself out of the hell that spawned it, launching itself into the air with a pair of batlike, threadbare wings that cast the arena in weird translucent shadows.

It landed among the detritus with a crunch that shook me again from my feet, and I lay on my back, staring up at a nightmare. It was the size of a building, reptilian and awful, with elongated, cruelly curling horns and rows of rotting teeth. Two blue orbs peered evilly from within its empty eye sockets, and its reeking stench made my stomach turn.

Things got worse, and quickly. The dwarven technomancer, her work complete, began directing traffic, using a combination of magic and her digitab to guide bits of machinery in the direction of the reanimated dragon. Pieces of appliances floated to mesh with the beast's ragged flesh, covering weak points and strengthening what looked to be an already powerful structure. The technomancer's spell, empowered as it was with the Scribe's life force, gave breath to the monstrosity, weaving its gristle and bone with pieces of technology from the Sigil's sanctuary to create something indescribably powerful.

I lay there, frozen, utterly horrified and useless. In dreamlike precision, I saw Agrid detach himself from the standing light, dextrously crawling up the dragon's haunches to nestle in between a bone-like ridge that had been reinforced with metal. He extended a hand, and the dwarf ran to take it, the entromancer hoisting her up to sit behind him.

The Destroyer searched the rubble below him with his eyes until he found me, hopelessly ineffectual beneath the monstrosity. His eyebrows rose, discernible even at this distance, then he turned forward, slapping the beast's neck with his spear. It roared, an unearthly, horrendous sound, and lurched into the sky with a beat of its powerful wings, blocking out the sun before turning to the west and away.

SEVEN

*Of course, we're willing to work with Aurichome,
just as we want to collaborate with each of our
neighboring nations, allied or otherwise. I'm
certain we can find common ground together.*
                -Marguerite Liu, NIGHT Inquisitor General

It took a few moments for us to gather our wits,
but once the specter of the dragon-thing had
disappeared past the lip of the amphitheater's
walls, it was as though a spell had been broken.
I jumped to my feet, pointing my pistol wildly in
search of the remaining assassins.

I didn't have far to look. Two cerucopters
shuddered to life from near the running track,
prepared for a hasty exit. Their ceridium-
powered engines spouting cold blue light, the
copters lurched into the air, sloughing off bits of
metal and equipment that had been used to
hide them from view.

I yelled, releasing a wave of pent up
adrenaline and a full clip of bullets that
bounced futilely off the copters' armor plating.
The vehicles pulled up over the lip of the
auditorium before following Agrid's path to the
west, the assassins within them mere shadows

behind tinted and reinforced glass.

I stood, panting, staring in the direction of the cerucopters' path and utterly spent. The gaping pit of the monster's egress yawned in front of me, a silent roar of earth, machinery, and destruction that reeked of rot and metal.

"Nightpath," Vasshka said gently, drawing my eyes back to the oval at the center of the pitch.

Gloric sat, his feet tucked underneath him, in front of the Sigil's broken form, tears streaming down his face. He held two pieces of the device in his tiny, swarthy hands, silently mouthing a prayer as he gently rocked on his heels.

The vacuum-shaped AI had been more than a resource to Gloric, I knew. The gnome had seen the Sigil as a miracle of technology in a world where the artificial intelligence experiment had long been proven to be farcical, and a mentor on Gloric's own path as a technomancer and Aurichome's Chief of Technology. His manipulation and destruction at the hands of Agrid and the Unaligned was a disturbing display of their power, but for Gloric, it was devastating and personal.

I walked unsteadily to the foot of the Scribe's pillow, the ancient human's body utterly desiccated and drained of its life force. It had slumped unceremoniously to the side of the pillow, the magic that had held it in stasis spent.

I leaned down to pick up the Scribe's tablet, which we had seen him use in constantly etching notes from the Sigil's auguries and other portents gleaned from patterns in the network. It was dusty from the spray of dirt and debris that occurred when the dragon-thing was vomited from the earth, but still functional, and surprisingly, accessible without any special credentials. I tapped a few buttons, scrolling through some of the Scribe's notes.

...Karthax reassured him. The Inquisitor General paced along the balcony rail, the sun casting his craggy face in radiance...

Thog'run stared ahead, his calculating eyes piercing the dim light of the underground audience chamber. A guard shifted nervously nearby...

"The question is not of cost, auromancer, but of ability," the holodisplay voice responded quickly, misunderstanding his question...

Kwame Daigan climbed, and kept climbing. The trail to the mountain fortress had been eroded by time...

Halyfax Dureaston stepped through the shimmering portal and appeared elsewhere. Whereas the sun had just been warming the tresses of her straight, strawberry blond hair, unfettered as they were from her heavy cowl, the rain in her new environs pelted her with dreadful force...

"Uh, Gloric?" I said nervously, tired beyond belief. "You may want to look at this."

The gnome snuffed, gently arranging the pieces of the Sigil on the ground and wiping his nose with a sleeve. He sidled over to the pillow, avoiding the Scribe's body and taking the tablet from me.

I surveyed the carnage while he tapped through the Scribe's notes. In a corner of the oval, Alina was using her terramancy to tend to Andrew's wounds, the giant staring stoically ahead while propping himself up against the back end of an antiquated vehicle. Buster and Celine stood companionably, watching the Pitcher do her work, while Vasshka paced irritably near the edge of the pit, which covered nearly half of the amphitheater, stopping abruptly at the verge of our little green oval. Thog'run III, the king's son, stood watching, quiet and analytical like his father.

"Where in the hell did that thing come from?" Doubleshot wondered out loud.

I shook my head, having no idea where to begin unraveling what had just happened. "Must have been some sort of technomancy," I offered.

Gloric coughed, clearing his throat. "It was," he said, his voice thick as he continued scrolling through the notes. "The Scribe recorded all of it, even throughout the spell that killed him. Agrid's technomancer – 'Ghela,' he calls her – enacted a spell using the Scribe's own power to reanimate a dragon and patch it up with the tech rubble around here."

"A dragon?" Alina said incredulously, looking up from her work. "A dragon," she repeated. "In Reno."

I thought of the entropic beasts that we had fought in the Presidio. They had suddenly become the *second* weirdest things we had seen in the past twenty-four hours.

"Seems like the Sigil hoarded more than just machines," Vasshka said.

Gloric nodded, looking intrigued. "The Scribe has recorded *everything* here," he marveled. "Karthax's attempted collusion with the king last year, Damara's politicking with the Unaligned, even our trip here this morning."

I pinched the bridge of my nose, trying to clear my head. "Does he say anything about what they're planning to do with the..." I searched for the right word. "Technodragon?"

Thog'run III cleared his throat, rubbing his neck and shoulders where he had been manhandled. "I overheard the Betrayer telling his dwarf to start her spell, right before you arrived," he said, his voice gravelly but higher in pitch than the king's.

Gloric tapped a few buttons, considering. "There's an encrypted message that was encoded by the Scribe just before we arrived. Let me see if I can – *ahh*, that's it," the gnome bobbed his head triumphantly.

"What does it say?" Alina walked over, Celine and a healed but gingerly walking Andrew in tow. Buster stayed by the vehicle, sniffing at old oil, rubber, and who knows what else.

The prince moved back a step as Andrew approached, more out of self-protection than fear.

"He's on our side now," Vasshka said unreassuringly, having known Thog'run III the longest among us. "Long story."

The prince nodded, staring warily at the giant, who did his best to smile disarmingly.

Something between understanding,

astonishment, and betrayal dawned in Gloric's eyes as he read the Scribe's message, mouthing something to himself.

"What does it *say*?" I repeated Alina's query impatiently.

The technomancer looked up at me, irritation mixed with his expression of shock. He held the tablet in front of him, which had a bunch of ones and zeroes on the screen.

"Can you read this?" he asked, pointing at the machine code.

"No," I said.

"Then give me a minute!" he clipped cantankerously. I exchanged a look with Alina, preferring the gnome to be angry over being despondent.

He drew in a long, shuddering breath, exhaling meaningfully. "Looks like the Sigil was a charlatan after all," he said at length, echoing Agrid's comment from when we had first entered the arena.

"What do you mean?" Alina asked, gently tousling Buster's hair as the wolf padded up to us.

The gnome smiled sadly. "He wasn't an AI after all," he explained. "The whole thing was a front for the Scribe's identity, to keep him out of the spotlight."

"The Scribe?" I prodded gently.

"Yes," Gloric said, looking down at the broken vacuum and then the Scribe's body, both lifeless. "He was the real Sigil, having programmed the..." he seemed struggling to find the most respectful word for what had been, until a minute ago, his mentor.

"Having programmed the *device* to issue his

messages," he concluded.

"I thought the Sigil's knowledge came from his ability to interface directly with the network as an AI," I said.

Gloric nodded. "Me too," he said, reading through the Scribe's message. "It seems as though the Scribe...the *Sigil*," he corrected himself, "was a technomancer himself, with no small amount of skill. What he wasn't able to accomplish through code, he plastered over with magic."

I rocked back on my heels, disbelieving. For the Sigil, a human, to have disguised himself on the network and in person as the Scribe, while still controlling the most powerful network on the planet, he would have to be extremely powerful indeed. And for the Unaligned to gain control over the Sigil's network and life force, to hide their actions from both Aurichome and NIGHT, and reanimate a dead dragon, made them utterly unassailable.

In the span of a heartbeat, things went from bad to unquestionably worse.

My digitab beeped, indicating a call waiting for me. I tapped it perfunctorily without looking.

"Yeah," I answered.

"Eskander?" it was Madge's voice, NIGHT's Inquisitor General contacting me on my private digitab.

"Yeah!" I said again, walking away from the group crowded around Gloric.

"What's your location?" she asked hurriedly. "We've got something going on in the undercity, and multiple bogeys converging on the Bay Area."

My spine went cold. "What kind of something?" I choked. "And what kind of bogeys?"

Madge's voice was noncommittal over the line. "Fires in the undercity," she explained, referring to the underrace warrens that stretched beneath San Francisco. "The aurics are spilling out from the smoke. And we don't have a visual yet on the aircrafts, but they're coming in pretty hot."

"What's going on?" Alina asked, concern etched on her angular features.

I shook my head, trying to think swiftly. "Madge," I said, "your Inquisitor – the one that attended Alina's ball game. Know the one?"

"Agent Drivas?" she asked, correctly surmising that I was referring to Damara. I shouldn't have been surprised that Madge knew all the names of the agents who reported up the chain to her.

"Yeah," I said. "Any idea where she's gone off to?"

There was a pause as Madge checked something. "She hasn't reported back since checking into Aurichome."

I nodded. "Figures. I think she's working with the Unaligned."

"Who?"

"I'll send you the details later. Can you get Gloric access to NIGHT's network?"

"*What*?!" she guffawed incredulously.

"What?" Gloric said, looking up from the Sigil's tablet.

"What's happening?" the prince asked Vasshka, his eyes shifting between us as he tried to piece together the conversation.

Andrew and Celine stood apart from the group, staring together at the Sigil's limp human form and the broken vacuum device.

"Nightpath's making a deal," Vasshka grunted appreciatively.

"I don't have time to explain, Madge," I said in my silkiest, most affably pleading tone. "Can you please just get him into the network?"

"Don't use that voice with me," the Inquisitor General rebuked. "Give me a reason to allow Aurichome's Chief of Technology access to the United States' *private* network."

I rolled my eyes. NIGHT was an autonomous paramilitary organization housed within the government's umbrella in name alone. Madge took her job a little too seriously, but as her friend and once colleague, I couldn't begrudge her.

"The Unaligned, or at least a splinter group of a new faction going by that name, have dusted the Sigil and taken over his network," I explained. "With it, they're more powerful than Aurichome and NIGHT individually, but not combined."

Madge was quiet, digesting the information. "They killed the Sigil?" she asked finally.

"Yeah. Sucked out his life force and used it to revive a dead dragon."

"I'm sorry, what?"

"We don't have *time*, Madge!" I snapped impatiently. "I'll ask Gloric to send you a report. Can you *please* get him access to the NIGHT network?"

Madge *tsked*, and I knew that I had put her in a terribly awkward situation, essentially asking her to open NIGHT's digital doors to their most bitter adversary in the form of Aurichome, on my word that there was a greater enemy to combat.

"Alright," she said begrudgingly. "But I'll ask my technicians to put protocols in place so we can shut him out in a blink."

"You're the best, Madge."

"Piss off, Eskander."

The line clicked, and I looked to Gloric, who was still reading the Sigil's tablet. "NIGHT's getting you access to their network. Can you connect it with Aurichome's and get back the Sigil's network from the Unaligned?"

"That's not how networks work, Nightpath," the gnome chided.

"You know what I mean," I said, exasperated. "Can you *do anything* to get a handle on whatever Agrid's people are doing?"

"I can try," he said slowly. "It'll take time, and probably some magic."

"Well, use magic," I said brusquely. "We don't have time."

"What's going on?" Alina asked. Dirt and blood smeared her pretty face, but she herself looked unharmed.

"Fires in the undercity," I said, "and some sort of aircrafts moving in on the Bay. The Unaligned are playing their hand."

"We've got to get going," she replied.

I nodded. "Gloric, can you get us a copter?"

"You're not a pilot," Vasshka pointed out.

"No," I agreed, "but she is." I pointed at Alina, who, during her time in the armed forces, had learned to fly military craft.

The Pitcher looked skeptical. "A propeller plane is quite different from a ceridium-powered copter."

"I'm sure you'll figure it out," I said confidently. "Most of these things fly themselves, anyway."

"Do they really?" Andrew asked, wide-eyed.

"They don't," Vasshka explained.

"Gloric, can you get us one?" I repeated.

The gnome glanced down dubiously at the Sigil's human body, ignominiously drained of life and discarded. I understood his reticence, and softened my voice.

"We'll give him a decent burial," I promised, looking to Andrew and Vasshka. "Can you two find a place for the Sigil away from here until help arrives to take him away?"

"No," Gloric said stubbornly. "He should be buried here, in his sanctuary."

I shrugged, consenting. "Whatever you think is best. Let's just clear the area for now."

The giant and dwarf gingerly picked up the Sigil's shrunken body, picking their way among the machines to find a place for it closer to the entrance and away from the technodragon's pit. Celine thoughtfully scooped up the pieces of the vacuum, following her brother while clutching them respectfully to her chest.

Gloric followed them with his eyes until the three were out of sight, then sighed and returned his attention to the Sigil's tablet, continuing to read. The prince watched us, and I had the distinct impression of my boss' son scrutinizing me to later report back to his father.

"Gloric," I said gently, if a bit insistently. "We don't have a lot of time here."

"He's provided instructions on how the Sigil's

network interfaces with others, and with all of the machines in the sanctuary," the gnome said, continuing to read the tablet and ignoring me. "It seems like he was expecting this to happen, and for someone to take his place."

"I can't think of anyone better," Alina spoke, understanding more quickly than me what was happening.

The gnome stepped over to the Sigil's cushion, brushing it tenderly free of dust and debris. Slowly, he sat on it, crossing his legs underneath him, looking uncomfortably out of place and insignificant on the big pillow.

"Looks like *you're* the Sigil now," Vasshka said as she and the others returned.

Gloric's eyebrows raised, the gnome clearly overwhelmed by the turn of events. He removed his keyboard from its case on his back, settling it into his lap while placing the Sigil's tablet on the pillow next to him.

The technomancer began to type furiously, muttering to himself as we looked on awkwardly, and some of us, impatiently. More than once, he extracted a ceridium tablet from a pocket, crushing it to power a spell that enhanced his control over the network, bypassing any barriers that stood in his way.

"I'm into the NIGHT network," he said at length, "and patching it into Aurichome. I still can't wrestle the Sigil's network from the Unaligned, but I can at least prevent *them* from getting into ours like they have."

I nodded. "That's great. And the copter?"

"Hang on." The gnome continued to type with a purpose, his eyes and fingers glowing blue as the magic augmented his power and control.

It took a few minutes, and Buster was the first to react to the buzzing. The wolf howled and skipped, agitated by whatever was headed our way.

They arrived so suddenly and with such coordination, I feared at first that the technodragon had returned. Blocking out the sun, dozens, if not hundreds, of drones appeared above the arena, whirring from every direction to join a growing flock of machines circling lazily around the sanctuary.

"Drones are back," Vasshka stated the obvious.

Here and there among the remaining tech detritus, a machine shook itself, convulsing to life as Gloric's network bid it to wake. Not a few drones lifted from the pitch to join the nimbus that had formed around the amphitheater. I was impressed.

A hole formed in the disc of circling, flying machines, wide enough for a black, pilotless cerucopter to pass through. The copter glided unwaveringly, touching down with a crunch several yards away from us amid the garbage.

"On loan from the Nevada dwarves," Gloric explained, his eyes still tinted with blue and his voice sounding like it was coming from very far away. His dusky forehead was furrowed and sweating with concentration. "You'll have to pilot it, however," he added, indicating Alina with flick of his chin. "I'm kind of busy here."

I moved towards the cerucopter, the urgency of the situation giving speed to my tired footsteps. Alina followed, delayed slightly after having to explain to Buster repeatedly that he was to stay with Vasshka, to which he reluctantly acquiesced.

A small hand tugged at my jacket, forcing me to turn around as I stepped to enter the copter. Celine was standing close to me, looking small, with a plaintive look in her dark eyes.

"Let me come with you," she said, her voice dissolving under the drone buzz and the copter's languidly swinging propellers.

"What? No," I said, a bit too roughly. I turned back to the cerucopter.

Celine clutched at my arm this time, her grip surprisingly strong. "Please," she pleaded, "I've...*seen* something."

I looked at her quizzically as Alina passed me to enter the copter's pilot seat and Andrew strode up to see what was the matter.

"What's this, hey?" he asked.

"She wants to come with us," I explained, trying to gently pry myself from Celine's grasp. "Says she's seen something."

"No way," he said with finality, his heavy accent making the words sound like *no, why.*

Celine, who had been reading our lips, looked cross with her brother. They began to sign furiously, and I used the opportunity to step over the copter's rail and into the metal interior.

"She says she's got to go with you," Andrew yelled as I took my seat. "Something about a vision of the future and all that. But I'm coming with!"

I shook my head, pointing back at Gloric, who was wholly absorbed in his task, and the crown prince, who would both be vulnerable even with Vasshka and Buster nearby.

"Stay and protect them," I shouted, bitterly

aware of the irony that I was asking him to be the guardian of his captive from the day before, but certain that he would be loath to try anything with his sister in my care. "I'll make sure she's safe," I added dubiously.

The big man looked over his shoulder at the new Sigil, tiny and exposed, then back at Celine, who stood patiently, a defiant look in her eyes.

Andrew sighed. "OK," he said, embracing his sister with a giant bear hug before turning away, joining Vasshka and the others and drawing his greatsword without looking back.

I helped Celine into the cerucopter, moving to make space for her in the small cockpit that doubled as a cabin and smelled of grease and steel. Alina was pushing buttons on her digitab, syncing it with the copter's navigation system.

I shut the cerucopter's side door, reducing the outside sound to a dull roar. "Can you get it to work?" I asked.

She pushed a button. "We'll see!"

The vehicle pitched forward, smashing through a refrigerator on the ground and driving my stomach into my feet. The copter bucked as Alina responded to stabilize it, then leaped into the air, too quickly for my liking.

Celine clapped delightedly like a child, and we levitated above the arena, being given a gruesome view of the pitch, which was rent in half with a gaping, bottomless pit that was still crumbling at the edges. Gloric glowed faintly blue below, with Buster barking up at us and Vasshka holding her hat as she shouted something at Andrew and Thog'run III.

The drones parted again as we reached their altitude, breaking their circle, presumably at Gloric's instruction, to arrange themselves in a phalanx formation, with our copter at the apex. At this vantage, I could see many of them equipped with various forms of weaponry, basic rotodrones mixed among more powerful ceridium-powered Merlin-class fliers.

Without a word, Alina turned us towards the west, speeding us away from the Sigil's sanctuary with an armada of drones at our back.

EIGHT

*We'll construct a partition. A barricade, around
the exterior of the undercity, and it won't cost
San Franciscans a penny. We'll ensure that
Aurichome pays for it in full, remuneration for the
turmoil and heartache they've visited upon us for
the past two decades.*
    -William D. Karthax, former NIGHT Inquisitor
General

The afternoon sun assaulted us as we flew west
towards San Francisco, bathing the Sierras
below in hues of gold and apricot. I had to
squint, even through the cerucopter's tinted
windows, to see in the direction of our flight
path, unwilling to tear my eyes from the horizon
and unable to make us move any faster.

The thrum of the drones was a muted rumble
behind and to the sides of us, their small forms
gilded by the sun and bobbing like geese in the
mountain wind. All of Northern California
stretched in front of us, cities dotting the tan
and brown landscape like flies among so much
sand.

We were silent as we flew, unsure of what to
expect but innately understanding the direness

of the situation. Agrid's technodragon and hell knew what else was on its way to San Francisco, while the Unaligned's revolt had begun to rear its nasty head in the predominantly auric undercity. I could only hope that the combined might of Aurichome and NIGHT, tremulous as their relations were with one another, would withstand whatever scheme the Unaligned had in store.

My optimism was deflated first by the scattered AR news feeds that began appearing on my digitab, and then by the sight of the Bay Area as we made our approach from the east. Utter chaos had descended upon the region, nonsensical and apocalyptic to my tired eyes.

For the second time in as many years, the city was on fire, black smoke tinted with flecks of angry red and orange against a backdrop of San Francisco's usual neon and concrete. Both layers of traffic were gridlocked moving in and out of the city, while NIGHT copters and other aircraft picked their way among the skyline attempting to restore some semblance of order.

As bad as the city looked, the North Bay in the direction of Aurichome appeared indescribably worse. Flashes of blue and crimson spattered the bank of evening fog clouds that had started to roll in, obscuring what looked like a terrible aerial fire fight.

"Take us towards Aurichome," I asked Alina instinctually, knowing in my gut that there was nothing that we could do at the moment for the aurics in San Francisco, and leaving them to the protection of Madge and her people.

The Pitcher swung us in a long arc to the north, our drone army banking to follow. Celine was pressed up against the starboard window, gawking out intently at the Bay and flashing skyline.

I tapped her gently on the shoulder, drawing the girl's childlike gaze away from the world outside of the copter. "Is this what you saw?" I asked, grasping at straws to understand what was happening. "In your vision?"

She shook her head firmly, reading my lips. "No."

I felt my brow furrow. "What did you see, then?"

"Nothing. I just wanted to come with you, and my brother wouldn't let me go without a reason."

I nodded, spent and resigned, letting my head rest for the briefest moments against the black leather cushion behind me. Within minutes, Alina's path cut us through the cloudbank towards the forests above Aurichome and into hell.

Military vehicles, of both aurikar and NIGHT origin, swooped and dipped, diving amidst unmarked aircraft and something more terrible in a battle for the skies above the auric nation. The firefight alone was terrifying in its intensity and pace, but my eyes were drawn to the abysmal threats that stalked the airspace like nightmares made flesh.

Four technodragons, similar in size to the one we had seen Agrid ride out of the Sigil's sanctuary, rent the sky, spoiling the strong ocean breeze with their filth. The dying afternoon sky, muted as it was by the surrounding clouds, washed them in hues of putrid brown and rust, broken claws and teeth glinting menacingly amidst rotting flesh and metal. Cold cobalt electricity skittered about their rotting skin, mingling with the bits of machine and metal that had been fused to their bodies to create a macabre display of deadly power.

The Unaligned had revived four of the technodragons, including Agrid's, and their intent to sow chaos had been made manifest.

"Oh," Alina said in dismay as we plunged into the battle.

Above Aurichome, the firefight raged, the king's modest air force being brought to bear against the new threat, cerucopters and fighters clashing with the Unaligned or railing pitifully against the gigantic beasts that tore through the air. Here and there, NIGHT aircraft lunged to the aid of the auric nation, grossly outmatched and outnumbered by a force that had been planning this assault for over a year.

Thog'run's artillery had been hastily deployed throughout the forest, firing from the ground below to deliver a glancing blow among the madness. The technodragons responded in kind, their serpentine forms glimmering awfully, rearing their metal-and-flesh heads at the behest of riders that straddled their ridged and bone-studded backs. Heaving their tattered, billowing torsos, they vomited blue, lightning-like rays of death, scoring the earth beneath and setting trees aflame. Utterly ignoring the military aircraft that pelted their impervious hides like gnats, they wheeled and circled, blasting the land with their ceridium-laced breath again and again.

"They're trying to expose Aurichome," I

realized with a startle, seeing the technodragons continue their pattern, slowly revealing the bedrock below the miles of scorched soil that provided the nation's ceiling.

"Piss," Alina cursed, hastily navigating us away from the slashing tail of one of the monsters.

As a passenger craft, we were woefully underequipped, but the drone army, at Gloric's direction, peeled away from their formation and joined the free-for-all like metallic arrowheads seeking their targets. They whirred through the carnage, firing unerringly at the Unaligned copters or dashing themselves against the bodies of the technodragons, attempting to unseat their more vulnerable riders.

Pandora had opened her box, and there was hell to pay. Aurikar, NIGHT, and Unaligned aircraft pirouetted and spiraled, the latter being harried by Gloric's drones as the sinewy technodragons scythed destructively through the forest. Our little copter jumped and jostled as Alina struggled to keep us out of harm's way.

"We've got to get out of here!" she yelled.

I nodded distractedly, my eye caught by a small cerucopter that rose through the carnage. It was one of the king's personal defense forces and of a newer design, two antigravity ceridium engines embedded in its winged undercarriage, obviating the need for propellers. It was black as a bat, with the blue and white symbols of Aurichome painted proudly across its wingspan, and making a beeline for the nearest technodragon.

My eyes flicked to the monstrosity, which supported two riders, and I instantly recognized

Agrid and his technomancer. The assassin's crimson coat flowed behind him wildly, and he stood among pieces of machinery that formed a makeshift harness affixed to the technodragon's spine, his spear glowing blue and crackling with power as he prepared to welcome the king's aircraft.

A window on the roof of the copter slid backwards into the black metal, exposing a heavily armored figure that struggled to contend with the whipping wind at our altitude. Even at this distance, his regal stature and enormous battleaxe were unmistakable.

It was Thog'run II, come to settle a vendetta long left to fester.

"Take us closer!" I shouted, grabbing Alina's shoulder while uselessly drawing my ceridium pistol.

The Pitcher looked up at me incredulously. "What? No!"

"It's the king!" I said, as though that should be reason enough to put ourselves in the reach of certain death.

"He's crazier than you are!" she countered, although she pivoted our copter to bring us closer to the action.

She wasn't wrong. As the king's aircraft neared the technodragon, it overshot the beast, flying over and around its lightning-laced carapace to swerve at the last moment back towards its original path. Thog'run used the maneuver to cover his movement from the technodragon's riders with the bulk of the copter, and then *jumped* from his perch, gripping the double-headed battleaxe in both hands over his head.

The trajectory of the aurikar copter sent the king sailing towards the head of the monstrosity, and the result was catastrophic. Thog'run II, his eyes wide and tusked mouth open in a horrible battle cry, struck the neck of the beast with his full might, the battleaxe sparking and spitting as its own ceridium core warred with the magical force that powered the technodragon. The weapon pierced the thing's disgusting hide, lodging itself into the technodragon's neck and causing Thog'run to hold on wildly as the beast bucked in what appeared to be distress.

I didn't have time to see what transpired next as our proximity to the main battle had attracted the attention of another technodragon, who was in between passes of delivering its devastating breath to the ground below. Dozens of rows rent the forest floor like evil claws, slowly but inexorably exposing the vulnerable auric city beneath. From our vantage, I could see the whisper of an outline of the very tops of buildings below, knowing that the people within would be scampering for safety from the tremors and clamor.

A drone zipped across our path, throwing itself at the technodragon as if to distract it from our copter. Alina jerked us to the side at the movement, dashing Celine against the interior of the copter with a yelp.

"Sorry!" the Pitcher apologized.

The young girl shook herself, steel in her eyes. She looked at me pointedly.

"Do you have ceridium?" she asked.

I nodded, absentmindedly handing her a couple of capsules as I futilely pointed my pistol at nothing.

The drone's attempted distraction did nothing, and several others followed it, careening into the technodragon only to burst into blue fire once within its aura. The beast curled towards us ponderously, almost languidly, its horrible visage turning to reveal the two riders on its back.

They were two women, one whom I recognized, and in that moment, I knew we were lost.

One was heavyset and broad-shouldered, a low auric wearing military fatigues and mantled with blue power that coalesced around her thick hands and forearms. Evidently a technomancer of some kind, she guided the beast's course through the air, lazily making its way towards us.

The second was Damara, exultant in her flowing Inquisitor's robes and eyes fixated on our cerucopter. I saw her arms wave in a mystic pass from a distance, feeling her magic penetrate my exhausted mind's weak defenses and hearing her voice in my head.

Stand down, Nightpath, it said in her silky voice.

I was too tired, bewildered, or terrified to respond, and something else entirely took over my body for what ensued. I had realized upon seeing Damara the extent of the plot that had taken hold of both NIGHT and Aurichome from within, a scheme years in the making that would thrust the Unaligned into unmatched power while simultaneously destroying its opposition.

Damara, and I dared not guess who else in

NIGHT, was still loyal to Karthax, jumping ship from the newly pluralist organization to fall in line with its xenophobic once-leader. From the Aurichome side, aurics seemed to be flocking to Agrid's standard, leaving the tenuous comfort of the king's sovereignty for some perverted sort of freedom under the banner of the Unaligned.

I had no idea who was pulling the strings, but perhaps emboldened by the king's sacrifice, foolishly believed that I could affect the outcome.

"Get us closer," I said, my voice echoing in my ears from a faraway place.

Alina looked at me disbelievingly for a second time. "I'm getting us *out* of here," she said forcefully, tapping on her digitab.

"Alina," I said, gently putting my hand over hers.

"What are you talking about?" she said, her voice hard and her eyes implacable.

I shook my head, at a loss for words.

"I'll protect him," Celine said supportively from behind me.

I couldn't help but smirk, envisioning Celine's pint-sized magic disintegrating under the full force of the technodragon.

Alina didn't find any humor in the girl's comment. "You'll get him *killed*, more like," she said, ignoring me as she turned the copter in a tight arc to retreat.

Her attempt at an evasive maneuver was feebly late. The technodragon gained on us quickly, its gigantic head leering behind us and poised to deliver its nasty lightning breath.

Without thinking it through, I shoved open the door of the cerucopter, hearing Celine hurriedly take up a chant behind me as I jumped from the vehicle, pistol in hand.

"Eskander!" I heard Alina yell as I crushed a ceridium capsule with my free hand, shadowstepping from the dubious protection of the copter to the back of the technodragon less than a stone's throw away.

I appeared in the giant harness that was bolted to its spine, surprising both Damara and the low auric technomancer as I landed in a crouch. I felt Celine's magic tickle my skin, some sort of spell that seemed to enhance my movements, making me feel as though my body was several seconds ahead of my mind.

I wasted no time, firing at the technomancer from point blank range as I drew my nightblade. The low auric slumped in her seat, dead, and the beast underneath jerked wildly as the connection was spent. Its magic control sapped, the monster jolted, following whatever infernal sentience that powered it.

I steadied myself against the harness, the technodragon's flesh damp and disgusting beneath my feet. Empowered as I was by Celine's chronomancy, I rode the beast's erratic movements as a sailor would navigate a rearing ship, slashing my nightblade crosswise at Damara's unprotected flank.

The Inquisitor was battle-hardened and savvy, tumbling backwards over the harness to grip it with one hand while pinching a ceridium tablet of her own. A bolt of fire sped from her fingertips towards my face, and I ducked, faster than thought because of Celine's spell.

The technodragon dipped and rose, shuddering and smelling of rot, and I struggled to hold on with both of my hands occupied with weapons. Instinctively dropping my pistol, I grabbed onto the harness, noticing yet another technodragon looming above us as we sprung forward in the air.

It was Agrid's, dark and terrible with no sign of the king in sight. I lifted my sword defiantly, ignoring Damara as she too turned to see what had drawn my attention.

The Destroyer's technodragon reared, its claws drawing backwards like an eagle closing in on its prey. It took in a long, phlegm-sodden breath, and expelled magic and lightning in our direction.

The beam widened to a girth of twenty feet across, enveloping us and the entire harness in its devastating blast. I felt power, lethal and absolute, wash over me, eliciting a deafening roar from the beast beneath me and obliterating everything else in its path.

A moment later, I felt nothing.

EPILOGUE

I startled myself awake, feeling as though I had fallen for an eternity and jolting into alertness as I hit the ground. My eyes were instantly blinded by some unseen light, searing into my skull mercilessly as my head pounded with pain.

I struggled to move, feeling hung over and sluggish, wresting my other senses to life to apprehend my location. My hearing returned first, filtering the sound of pebbles against stone and the heaving of a great bellows. A bird chirped somewhere nearby, along with the murmur of voices that I didn't recognize.

I smelled fire, or smoke, and panicked momentarily, suddenly remembering the fight above Aurichome amid drones and technodragons. I stumbled to a crouch, feeling my nightblade in my hand, and immediately vomited from a wave of vertigo. I slumped back to the ground, passing out for another eternity.

When I awoke for the second time, I was in a sitting position, uncomfortably situated against a rock or something hard to help me avoid drowning in my own spittle. My head was still throbbing but tolerable, and I opened my eyes to see blurry shapes in front of me.

I looked down, vaguely registering the nightblade at my side, veined with blue against the grassy earth underneath. Slowly, I took in my surroundings, blinking against the harsh sunlight overhead.

I was in a forest, or rather, in a large clearing within a forest, trees ringing the edge of a dell that was scorched and pocked by time. Scraggly weeds and short grass filled the clearing, easing what was an otherwise barren stretch of land.

Two hazy figures hovered before me, backdropped by a large vehicle of some sort. They waited patiently as my eyes adjusted, whispering among themselves.

One of them was a man, ancient but fit, wrapped in a wool cloak and with skin the color of night. The other was a woman I hadn't met, but looked like someone I had known a long time ago.

Seeing that I was rousing, the man took notice of me, his boots crunching the ground underfoot as he approached. I struggled to grab my nightblade but couldn't find the strength, and resigned myself to whatever fate awaited me.

The man crouched to be at eye level with me, his features hard but kind, and his long ears belying his high auric heritage. I looked past him to the woman, who was human, and aging, although not as old as the auric in front of me.

The dark auric patted the ground next to him disarmingly, smiling gently. His teeth were white and his voice was heavily accented as he spoke.

"Hello, Eskander," he said, his voice strong

and mellifluous despite his age. "My name is Kwame Daigan. You know Celine," he nodded to the woman behind him, "and this is Zzethromandus."

I looked past the auric at the human woman, not understanding. She looked as though she could be the Alyawarres' mother, sharing some of the same aboriginal features of Celine but decades older than the young girl.

Behind her, the vehicle stirred, and I saw its true form for the first time. Cold black scales shimmered in the daylight, brilliant in their prismatic opalescence, covering a beast that was almost as big as a cerujet. Its gigantic wings fluttered, casting the clearing momentarily in shadow, until it settled back on its hind claws, expelling a smoky breath through its nostrils as it pierced me with a green-eyed gaze.

I froze, fear and adrenaline overcoming my nausea and lethargy.

"What," I said, my mouth suddenly dry. "Where are we?"

The woman called Celine shooed at the dragon, irritated that it had startled me. She walked over to join the auric in front of me, and power followed her like a cloak.

"It is roughly thirty years beyond your time on this world," she said, her voice as thick as I remembered it and eyes brimming with a magic that was palpable as she drew near.

"It's what?" I said stupidly, uncomprehending.

The woman smiled knowingly. "We've been waiting for you," she replied, her voice confident and warm. "We've brought you to the future to heal the past.

"Come," she continued, motioning to the auric to help me stand. "There is much to share, and even more to do."

ABOUT THE AUTHOR

M. S. Farzan was born in London and grew up in the San Francisco Bay Area. He has written and worked for high-profile video game companies and editorial websites such as Electronic Arts, Perfect World Entertainment, Modus Games, and MMORPG.com, and has served as the Community Manager for games like *Dungeons & Dragons Neverwinter* and *Mass Effect: Andromeda*. He has trained in and taught Japanese martial arts for over fifteen years and has a Ph.D. in Cultural and Historical Studies of Religions.